FINGERLESS

IAN DONNELL ARBUCKLE

ACKNOWLEDGEMENTS

I'm grateful to the following for helping me build this: Lis, Mark, Justin, J, Angie, Annemarie, Phil, Leonard, Vic, T, Dad, Mom, Daniel, Joel, Bob, Gail, JC, and M/G. I'm in their debt for their influences on my life and my efforts.

ISBN: 978-1-938349-12-6

Library of Congress Control Number: 2013904564

Layout and Design by Mark Givens
Artwork by Ian Donnell Arbuckle

Printed in the USA

First Pelekinesis Printing 2014

www.pelekinesis.com

Fingerless

Ian Donnell Arbuckle

For Liam

Prologue

Junior year of high school, the night after our cross-country teams got back from State, Shasta threw a party. She had a great house for it, up on the flats, just out of town, surrounded by acres of orchard land. As children, she and I had invented labyrinths in the orderly rows of apple and pear, pretended at being lost, at saving one another from the beast that prowled in the darkness. We never did agree on what the beast might be.

It was going to be a good party, a long one. Twenty-odd of us on the guys' team, more than that on the girls', and that added up to most of the school population for ninth through twelfth. Shasta decided the theme was going to be "Come As You Aren't." It took some explaining, but basically Shasta wanted everyone to show up as their own opposites. I helped her shop for her costume. Blonde hair dye, tank tops, jeans tight enough to give her a little tummy bulge where one didn't belong, bad jewelry, and lots of gum since we

were seventeen and couldn't get away with
Marlboros.

Up until that night—after the teams had gotten
home from the meet, piled out of the bus, and scattered so we could come back together—I hadn't quite
figured out what I was going as. I ran cross-country
and track, but I couldn't guess what the opposites of
those were. My grades were all right, so maybe a
slacker. I didn't have much school spirit; maybe, I
thought, I should go as the ASB president. What's
the costume for that?

I took a quick shower while thinking. My time at
State had been horrible; my legs were the sorest they
had been since first practice. Side effects of the meds,
I told Coach Dale. No biggie, he said. Boys placed
third, anyway. Girls took first.

Looking at the blur of my reflection in the fogged-
up mirror, I thought maybe I would go in my street
clothes. My jeans, team hoodie, scummy sneakers.
Splash on a little of my brother Victor's cologne.
Bring along a set of free weights?

"What are you supposed to be?" Shasta would ask.

"Just some dude," I would reply. And then what?
Explain things to her right then, with her cheeks red
from grinning at friends, her brain set on shallow
paths of here and now. Let her stare, confused, and
then brush me off or grab my hand and let me tag

along, forgetting about it, only later to come back and say she was bummed I didn't dress up for her party.

"I did," I'd say, too chicken to go on. "Smell the cologne?"

I flicked on the bathroom's overhead fan and wiped the mirror with my towel. I came into focus from the waist up. There was an alternative. Just thinking about it made my heart speed up, like knowing the tough answer in class. I wrapped the towel around me, belly-button height, and went to the room I had shared with Victor ever since I graduated from the crib.

Victor and I still slept in the bunk bed Dad had built when we were kids. It was the only way either of us had any space for a desk. Up until middle school, we had fought over who got top bunk, switching every so often on a schedule based on how tired of arguing Mom was at the time.

Each of our desks—wooden planks balanced on mismatched filing cabinets—had one locked drawer. Because of the way they fit into the corner, we couldn't both have our drawers open at the same time. This had caused no end of knuckle-bumps and indian burns over who could get into their toy drawer first. Around when Victor got into the sixth grade, he had asked Dad to put a lock on his drawer to keep me out of it. That was fine by me. Now I could get into my toys whenever I wanted and Victor would have to wait until I decided to go play with them outside before he fished out his key from wherever and unlocked his stuff.

I remember searching high and low for that key. It's hard to have secrets in a room that size, but it didn't turn up in any of his usual hiding places. Eventually, after giving up the search several times, I had a great idea. I asked Dad to put a lock on my drawer, too. The next day, when I got home from school, there was a key taped to the wall above my pillow. First I tried it on my lock. It worked, but back then I didn't have much I needed to hide. Then I tried it on Victor's drawer. The locks were the same. Cheap jobs from the local hardware store, not much more than the sort you'd find fastening a diary shut.

Victor's drawer was full of glossy magazines, unlabeled VHS tapes, and a Post-It note covered with web addresses for porn sites. I was kind of disappointed. Not as much as he would be when he tried his key out on my lock, though. I filled my drawer up with dirty clothes I picked up off the floor and topped it off with one of Mom's Avon magazines about lipstick.

Not so different now, I thought, closing the door behind me. The locks were still on our drawers. Victor hadn't bothered fastening his shut for years. Mine I kept locked any time I was out of the room, but not because of Victor, who probably still had his key somewhere.

I usually wore my key around my neck on a chain, like a cross, a reminder. Today, I had left it under the tattered corner of carpet by the door so it wouldn't get lost at the meet. I retrieved it and unlocked my drawer. Dug past the layer of socks. Beneath them were a pair of plain cotton panties, a white bra, a long denim skirt and a summer blouse. A pair of thin, silicone breast pads lay flat on the bottom, next to a slim case of basic makeup I had gotten as a free sample from a Mary Kay ad.

Clothes, then hair and makeup. I had shaved my legs thats morning already. "Cuts down on wind resistance," I had joked to my teammates. The hardest part was making a believable set of breasts. The silicone pads only did so much, and rags or socks were too lumpy behind them. Over the last few months, I had developed my own method, using a set of rubber exercise bands wrapped, knotted, and folded to make a convincing A-cup, as long as no one tried to peer down my shirt. Better than folded socks. That's why the blouse had a high neckline, only a slight V at the hollow of my throat. The exercise bands stayed in place pretty well; I could even run, if I wanted, but had never tried since there wasn't much room to cut loose between the desks and the bunk bed.

There was a roll of medical tape in one of my unlocked drawers. We used it for sports injuries, mostly, as far as Mom and Dad knew. I made a few short strips and carefully bound up my penis in as low a profile as possible. Hurts, like maybe being cut with hot tin snips might, if you do it wrong.

Under the panties—*pantettes* is a better word, more accurate, less naughty, more grandma—and the skirt, no one could tell if I'd done it wrong or right, except by how I walked, strutted, hobbled, whatever.

I fought the urge to *sneak* back into the bathroom, keeping my head up and smiling; if Mom or Dad caught me, I could just tell them the truth. I'm dressing up to go to Shasta's party. The girls got first. No, I didn't beat my personal best, but I got close. Yeah.

Still, I felt safer with the bathroom door closed behind me. I used Mom's curling iron to straighten out my hair, then add an outward flip at the tips. It made me look like I was from the seventies, but it was the only thing I had practiced. I didn't do much with my face. Some eyeliner, a neutral, shimmery shadow, and, my favorite part, lips just a shade darker than the brown skin around them. I glanced at my nails. No time, but at least the grime from the track had gone down the shower drain.

The mirror gave me a kind look I couldn't return for long. Time to go. The only thing missing was a pair of shoes. I dug mismatched flip-flops out from under the bunk bed, finally found mates. They were made for men. Thick soles, lots of traction. We had called them thongs until seventh grade when I learned about women's underwear. Even if I had had a thin-soled, smooth pair—maybe in white, or anything not-black—my feet weren't the most feminine. Which way would look more out of place, I wondered.

There I was. No curves but invented ones. Shoulders fit poorly to the seams of the blouse. Killer makeup job, though. Delicate restraint.

Mom and Dad were watching TV together. Mom had two shows running at the same time. Jumping back-and-forth, picking up snatches of two plots. Dad had his arm around her shoulders.

"Going to the party," I said, breezing past behind them. Dad raised his free hand and gave me a wave over his shoulder with the three fingers he had left.

The road up to Shasta's place was packed the last half mile or so, cars parked, abandoned every which way on both shoulders, narrowing down to one lane. I pulled up at the end of the line and got out. It pisses Shasta off when I do that, take the first spot I see. Sometimes we day trip to the mall in Spokane. There, I grab whatever's free. Saves time, I say, since we don't chug around in circles waiting for someone up closer to pull out. Takes more time, she argues, and her shoes are never good for walking.

My not-so-girlish feet crunched over gravel and twigs blown off from the slash piles. A couple of the orchards near the house had been ripped out. Not because of disease or anything, like I figured it was.

Turned out they just stopped being profitable. Nobody wanted Washington apples when Japanese were so much cheaper. It ended up costing more to keep the orchards alive and growing than the orchardists could get from selling their crop. So, out they came, leaving behind huge piles of broken limbs, whole trunks, and tangles of root systems.

A couple of these piles flanked either side of Shasta's driveway. As I approached, I could see some guys climbing around on one, kicking back wherever they found perches, like lost boys. The tips of their cigarettes hopped, sputtered like weary lightning bugs. Victor hung toward the bottom, leaning with both his elbows behind him against what used to be the topmost branches of an apple tree. He was smoking a hand-rolled.

Someone higher up gave a cat-call, someone I couldn't see.

I gave Victor a huge grin. "What aren't you supposed to be?" I asked.

He shook his head. "Smokin," he said. "Drinkin." A Coors tall boy balanced in a Y beside him. "You've got lipstick on your teeth," he said.

"Part of the costume. No fighting." I turned to leave.

"No promises."

When I was out of sight of him, I wiped at my teeth. My fingers came away clean.

A nerd with taped-up glasses and a girl in football pads and a jersey were making out on the front porch. They didn't notice me. I picked around the squeaky spots on the wooden steps. At least I wasn't the only one dressed up. A jagged ball of apprehension grew in my stomach, shifting with each step, digging sharp points into my nerves whenever it wanted. It felt strangely like Christmas morning used to when I was a little kid. Waking up at two in the morning, spending hours flat on my back, with all the potential presents getting me giddy, twitching. Or maybe there's just one shape that nervous takes.

I brushed past a set of wind chimes, discs of sliced agate, and into a chamber of alcohol fumes. Music shook the walls, each downbeat setting a brief, sympathetic rattle in the family photos hanging at eye level. The closet overflowed with coats. Fashionably late, I thought, catching on just a bit too late that my mouth twisted in a grimace when I did. A sophomore—fast kid, made varsity sooner than anyone else in his grade—tripped from somewhere out of sight and sprawled across the hall in front of me, laughing his eyes out. Drunk out of his mind. Wearing a skirt. He spotted me, my wry smile not yet smoothed away, and choked on something.

"Ha, ha, gross!" His voice cracked a bit. He let his head fall back against the carpet and sputtered like an old car. His costume didn't fit at all right on him. Plain boxer shorts under his skirt, which probably belonged to his sister. He had already wet himself a little bit.

Shasta's laugh cut through the thick, hot air. I ventured out into the hallway and peered into the sunken living room. There she was, trashy as hell, in the outfit we had picked together, sitting slant-wise in an easy chair, legs crossed delicately at the ankles, holding a flute by its stem with a finger and thumb, smiling the smile that was all hers. Her eyes flicked up when I entered and she gave a long squeal. Launching herself out of her chair, she spilled a little of whatever was in her glass, and then she had her arms around me.

"Oh my god! You look so great!" She couldn't contain herself, did a cheesy little dance. "Your makeup is amazing!"

The rest of the room had given over to hysterics, mostly. The girls seemed to like my get-up. A couple of the guys gave each other looks.

"Oh, wow, I wish I could do my eyes like that." Shasta poked at my cheeks, pulling them down. She was a little drunk, a little more touchy-feely than normal. I caught her hands and kissed their tips. A brief, disengaging moment, which I could almost guarantee wasn't the same for Shasta as it was for me.

However it felt to her, it passed, and then I was sitting, knees together, on her chair, with her draped over my lap. It was mostly us juniors and seniors hanging out in the living room for the next few hours. The frosh and sophomores on the teams were outside, some of them sitting in the hot tub, some of them playing heavy-handed touch football. We talked about the meet, about scores, about who was going to do track next season. Laughing, buzzed, all about us.

I didn't drink much, but what little I did went straight to my bladder. Some of us were getting sleepy, lethargic, dozing off on shoulders. One guy had dressed up as a pirate. He said it was like celebrating Halloween. I didn't understand until Shasta explained that he was a Jehovah's Witness. A girl in a jail uniform had her chin hooked around his neck, kind of from behind. Perched like a parrot. After a few lulls in the conversation, I scooted Shasta out of my lap, said I had to go pee.

The bathroom was vacant. It looked as if it had been crowded earlier, though. Some puke on the floor, streaked, hurriedly wiped up with toilet paper. Weed smoke, thin, invisible, but definitely there. I shook my head—a gesture meant just for myself—and caught a glimpse of it in the mirror.

I hadn't brought the little makeup case, so I couldn't do any touch-ups. My skin shone with sweat and oil. No good under fluorescent lights. I turned away from the mirror, put the seat down on the toilet, and sat. Carefully, I undid the tape and let enough pressure off for the pee to escape. Pretty sweaty down there, too; so much so that the tape refused to restick when I was done.

It was either make do with the few Band-Aids I dug out of the medicine chest, or toss the idea. I crumpled up what was left of the tape and chucked it into the little, overflowing rubbish bin behind the sink. From what I could tell, looking down at myself and smoothing my skirt, you couldn't see much of it. As long as it didn't get a mind of its own, I'd be all right. I left without getting the mirror's opinion. Sprayed a bit of air freshener behind me.

Shasta had drug the conversation back to a lively place when I got back to the living room. Everyone half-awake, but all the more ready to giggle for it. It's a shitty thing to admit, but I hate it when people laugh without me. The sound makes a kind of bubble. Once the laughter starts, it's as hard as hell to get yourself in, edgewise. I leaned against the wall and smiled and waited for a chance to sneak back.

It took long enough that my feet started to get sore, even in the sensible shoes I had picked. Curfew hit for a couple of the hangers-on; bit-by-bit, the living room emptied. Even the younger kids outside had either quieted down or left without saying goodbye. Shasta spoke quietly with another girl, Arabekah, or something like that. I couldn't really hear them, and it still wasn't a good time to come back into the room. Finally, Arabekah yawned. I slipped down the step and over to Shasta's chair, touching her lightly on the back of the neck. Arabekah asked if she could stay the night. That was it. I had made it through the party.

I squeezed into the chair beside Shasta. She pulled herself to her feet to make sure there were spare towels for Arabekah to use. I waited in the living room. Silence cranked up its intensity, making up for the lost time it had been filled up with all of us. I listened to it, felt strangely and selfishly respectful.

Shasta padded down the hall. She paused on the threshold to look at me for a moment.

"Are the pills not working?"

I shrugged. "Too early to tell," I said. "The side effects hit right away, but the doctor said that the depression never vanishes overnight."

"Makes sense," she said. I let the silence build again. Shasta was used to these one-two-three exchanges with me, when I wasn't feeling talkative. She'd ask a question or prompt me. I'd respond, briefly, or wordlessly. She cap it off, have the last word, not to somehow win, I thought, but so I didn't have to hear myself echo afterward.

Something came over me. "Sorry," I said.

"Come on." She held out a hand, kept it out while I came to her side. "Time for bed." She smiled perfectly. Then she reached up and tweaked one of my fake boobs and giggled.

"Hey! Don't mess with my mosquito bites."

She hummed a couple of bars, then faked it: "A mosquito, my libido."

Her room was on the second floor. She led me up the stairs, past the gauntlet of framed pictures, from school, from sports, from grandparents; in each one, in the low-light reflections, I saw her leading a stranger. Not enough of a stranger, sometimes, and sometimes too much of one.

I followed her into her room and switched off the lights behind me. We found each other in the dark after a false start. Our costumes came off, carefully, one garment at a time, trading my hands for hers, and hers for mine after every one. A door slammed downstairs. The shower came on in the bathroom, just across the hall.

"Cover my mouth," Shasta whispered, kissing me afterward. We lay down, her beneath me. I ran one hand the length of her body, propped myself up with the other. She guided me into her, again after a couple of false starts, since I wasn't hard enough. She let out a moan; I slipped my free hand over her mouth, which made her breathing quicken.

Partway through, she bit at the flesh of my thumb. I pulled away, but the moment I did she groaned, loud enough to hear across the hall. I kissed her, heavily, letting my weight crush her as best I could. We breathed through our noses. After a while, I stopped completely.

We rolled apart, my arms sore from supporting my weight. Shasta leaned over to her bedside table and switched on the lamp there. She grabbed a box of tissues and mopped up between her legs. Then, smiling, she rolled over to face me.

And burst out laughing.

"What?"

Coherency came slowly. "Your lipstick's all smudged." She wiped at her own mouth. "It's all over me. You didn't use a sealer, did you?" She wiped one of her stained fingers over the tip of my nose.

Tears fell from my lids; I bent to cover them. They were unexpected, but looking back I can hardly believe I hadn't felt them coming. The weatherman sees thunderheads in the muggy summer heat. The retiree on his front stoop knows when the drought will break by the violence of the crickets. Then the storm cracks the sky, the heat rises up and out of the world, the rain drags a sheet of mist down over the plains.

"What's wrong? Baby?" Shasta might as well have never slipped a grin in her life.

So, cradling my head in her lap, she listened to me—not the side effects of the Effexor, not the falseness I wore like a shell around school, but me—put into words the very first time what I had learned, wordless, in the last few years. I messed it up, big time, but she kept listening. I tell myself that she listened and listened, except that the one thing I remember the most is how it started, my first reply:

"I'm not even a man," to which she said:

"Yes you are, baby. Hush."

One, two, three.

Part One: Young Husks

1

I shook out my hair and for a moment was so happy. Gracie had done a beautiful job. I could still smell the salon on my skin, my hands and face, from yesterday. When Victor had told Gracie about me, she had just about died happy, he said. That was a new one on me. But Gracie had been excited to meet me, excited to get me into her chair and come after me with her scissors, razor, bottles, fingers, tin foil, you name it. All the time babbling about how cute it was going to be, and how rough it must have been growing up ("Nah. Victor was all right as a kid.") and how she couldn't believe how much courage I had.

By the end of the session, she had earned herself a big tip, and I saw the hint of a woman in the mirror.

Alone in my apartment's tiny bathroom, the hint had turned into a whisper. My hair was perfect, dark with touches of subtle highlight, exaggerating the natural, loose curl, but it framed a squarish jaw, thin lips, thick eyebrows. There would have been dark stubble, if the combination of the spiro and my recent teary-eyed applications of wax hadn't taken care of it. Electrolysis sounded like a better option, or lasers, or something scientific. For now, my hormones worked to plug things up at the source, and my own two hands cut down anything missed.

I reminded myself that this was the first day, not the last. I took a deep breath then got dressed, pits opening in my stomach now and then without warning. During the two weeks I had taken off of work, I had perfected my morning routine. Up at 6, pills, shower, shave with great care, clothes, hair, makeup, breakfast, brush teeth, done by 7. 6:50, usually. That left me with forty minutes to walk to the hospital, where I worked in the basement with the shelves and shelves of patient charts. It usually took me thirty; less if it was raining and I hurried.

I used to love the smell of rain. It could toggle a bad day. Everything could be crap, but a few seconds in front of an open window in the middle of a downpour or a sprinkle or even just the threat of rain on the breeze and I could hang on for hours. Technically I live in a desert, with an annual rainfall of less than three inches. Not exactly what you picture when you think of Washington state. Blame it on the Cascades; they cast a long, dry shadow.

I'm kind of grateful for it now. The smell of rain, which used to revive my days gone dead, took on a rough change a couple of weeks after I started myself on spironolactone. The side effects present much faster than the intended ones, and one of the more obscure possibilities with anti-androgens is that your sense of smell may be temporarily enhanced. Headaches, nausea, cottonmouth, all that I had gone through with other meds, back when I was just trying to treat the symptoms of depression. This was new. A super power, I told myself, kind of feeling light in my head just because it was so new, so different. I hoped that the brand new side-effects foreshadowed a new set of intended effects.

It rained the day I went back to work. The last thing I did before leaving was put in the paperwork to have my name changed in the HR system. The days didn't feel like a vacation so much as those last shreds of summer before school started back up. I passed them alone and they left without much bother.

Then, on the day I went back to work, everything was dark. The clouds were so heavy, cloaking the morning so fully that I thought my alarm clock had busted, leapt ahead a few hours. I got ready with all the lights on, running through the routine again.

My throat clenched as soon as I stepped outside. A light rain had already fallen and ceased, its drops looking like a heavy dew all over the apartment complex's short-mown grass. It was as if I could smell every microscopic creature in the soil and plants, or more like their dead members, things rotting. Even the living things smelled old, crusty, and unkempt. The difference between the smell of dog and wet dog. I realized, nose wrinkled, that what I used to love was the smell of sterility, of the rain tamping down the other smells of nature.

As I walked it started raining again. It came down as a mist. By the time I made it the four blocks to the hospital, I thought maybe I could smell some long-dormant fungus sprouting on my coat. Silly thought, because the coat was brand new. It got me thinking that if you were a super hero you'd be better off having been one from birth. Gaining new powers partway through life is enough to throw anyone out of whack. Plus can you imagine coming out to your parents as a demigod? "Mom, Dad, I don't want you to freak out, but—"

Best way to unleash a secret, really.

My hair didn't survive the thorough soaking, and before long it looked like I was sporting wet-look dreads. Not, as someone in the know might say, complementary to my facial form. I left a trail of puddles from the basement door to the unisex bathroom we shared with maintenance and housekeeping.

After a brief appraisal in the mirror, I pulled a hairbrush out of my purse—both purchases I was proud of. At the end of each stroke, a short cascade of rainwater pattered on the tile floor, having been pushed ahead of the brush's teeth. Someone tried the door handle and then knocked. I tilted my head this way and that. A curtain of brownish hair stuck first to one side of my face, then the other, glued wetly, only breaking loose and swinging across heavily when the angle of my face became too severe. Each time passing in front of my nose drawing behind it a sick smell of my body's oils, sour ones.

I tried a little styling while still damp, but it seemed like my hair had reached its peak femininity for the morning. Maybe Gracie, Victor's girlfriend, could have done a bit of something with it, sure. Just a twist here or maybe a couple of barrettes if I didn't mind going sixth-grade-chic for the day. I had a lot to learn and my purse had only my wallet, with its wallet chain I hadn't bothered to disconnect yet, a tube of lip balm, a couple of wet wipes, and a big space where my hairbrush fit neatly. Shasta had the muscle memory to take her hair in one fist, a clip in the other, and with a swish more like sleight-of-hand than styling her messy yellow curls would be at least half-caged. The motion itself had been improbably sexy, once upon a time; now it made me jealous.

No one could say that I was a sight for sore eyes. More like the sight from which sore eyes are born, like bright lights or impossible combinations of color.

I pulled my purse's zipper closed after replacing my brush. From outside the door, someone said: "Done now?"

I unlocked the door and slipped out. Leaning against the painted cinderblock wall, one of the older maintenance guys—he had celebrated twenty years with the hospital a couple of months past—chuckled in my direction. "You din't wash up, kiddo." Some people joke all around and expect you to just somehow know when they're putting you on or are really put off. I usually just act like they're joking; I wish I wouldn't. I'd rather make the mistake of taking a joke seriously than the other way around. I blew out a bit of a laugh back at him.

Just before the door closed behind him, he called out: "Hey! Din't hear no flush either." My shoes squeaked something awful on the grungy tile leading to the medical records office. I thought about taking them off, because they pinched my baby toes pretty bad, too, but I didn't want to put too much wear on my nylons—still afraid of the phantom called a Run—and besides the hallway was full of puddles made by other people's shoes, which meant the carpet in the office was probably just as damp.

Even knowing it was coming, I gagged as I opened the door. The moisture had loosed whole colonies of something foul-smelling and invisible. The hospital's basement used to be all gravel floors and butcher's racks for storing files. A couple of years before my time, they had paved over with the cheapest concrete they could find, with the cheapest labor on offer. The end result was porous and uneven, and the patchwork linoleum and indoor/outdoor carpet didn't do much to hide or protect it. There were notes of sulfur, wood rot, worn arch supports, and more, but the worst was the somehow rotten, wet dog smell of old carpet shampoo. We were not well-shielded from whatever lurked beneath the Earth in that place.

I made my way to my desk carefully, trying not to touch any of the wet spots and accidentally kick loose another pocket of the smell, imagining the stench like the puffs of spores from summer-dried mushrooms. "Hi, Lita," said Mary, sitting at her desk across the aisle from me. She smiled wide enough for me to see a flake of onion pinched in her teeth from the cafeteria's breakfast burrito. "It's really coming down, isn't it?"

"It sure is." I note these pieces of normalcy, as dull as they are. We've shared these exact same words, in the same order, the same cadence, Mary and me. Only things different were this time my nose was all scrunched up, and that Mary's smile used to be more subdued.

I set my purse on the desk next to me and started into my work, no ritual. A backlog of dictations had built up over the weekend, as usual. Transcription is a good job, if you can get it. It's one of those ones they're always trying to sucker you into on the Internet, because it sounds so easy. Buy our eight week training course. Work from home at your own pace.

It had gotten my attention, anyway. I dreamed about working in my jammies, picking my clients from far-flung corners of the world. Freelancing. I love that word; it's powerful and open.

Things didn't turn out quite like that, of course. The training course was a bit of swindle, but at least I learned to look hard for the word "accredited" in any future schooling. I managed to pick up enough to land and ace the interview for a part-time position at the hospital, comforted that the interviewer kept using the phrase "on-the-job training."

I had been there two full years, and even though my manager hadn't yet authorized pajama day I did at least get a paycheck. No benefits, but I didn't bear much bitterness at that after I learned they wouldn't have covered what I needed anyway. The cash was enough of a benefit.

Most of the time—the dry times—I liked it down there in the basement. I could spend the whole day in my little corner, across from Mary, headphones on, listening to how and why my neighbors got sick or beaten up, writing it all down. I learned more than a little bit about medical terminology and practice, so if I had a headache at the end of the day I kind of felt as if I had earned it. The one big downside was that I couldn't listen to music while transcribing.

My skin crawled underneath my damp clothes. Water sluiced, oily, around the earphones when I put them in. I pulled up the queue from the emergency department and started into a three-minute summary of a little girl who had had an allergic reaction to a spider bite.

My co-workers trickled in over the next half hour, peeling off coats, stamping their shoes. Each one caught my eyes and smiled. Business as usual. Joy, my manager, was the last to arrive. She carried her work shoes in one hand, clomping down the aisle in a pair of knee-high rubber waders. I imagined I could hear the thick soles squishing over the spongy carpet, even through the brash Southern accent of the locum ER doc stuttering through my headphones.

Joy sat heavily in her chair and yanked off the waders, replacing them gingerly with the bargain black flats she favored. In an instant, she changed from fisherman's wife to prim and proper auntie. Up on her feet again, she padded from cubicle to cubicle, checking in. When she got to mine, she just stood and pretended to read a sheet of paper until I found a stopping spot and pulled the wires from my ears.

"How are you doing, Lita?" she asked. Her hair had been gray for decades. She had a short cut, kind of butch if you saw it from behind. If you were on her good side, she was a saint, the kind that intercedes on your behalf. I had heard stories of staff—even doctors—who had gotten on her bad side. None of the stories came directly from her.

"I'm good," I said, and gave her a smile. I had practiced both the phrase and the expression in front of the mirror, modulating my voice as best I could, keeping my big teeth demurely hidden behind my too-thin lips.

Joy dropped her voice. "Still Hernandez, right?"

"HR didn't get the forms to you?"

"I guess not."

"Oh, OK. Yep. Still Hernandez."

Joy nodded, filing the info away. She had been born to keep records. "I tried to help out as much as I could while you were gone, but there's probably a bit to catch up on."

"It's good," I replied, not meaning to be brusque. I just hadn't managed to practice my tone and timbre on much of my vocabulary. I could tell it didn't bother Joy. She nodded and returned to her desk, not one for spending much excess time on words. I wish I could have said as much for the docs I was transcribing.

I put off my filing as long as possible. The shelf of recent charts stood right next to the office door, in full view of everyone over their low cubicle walls. After an hour of typing, I had to go sort transcriptions into their proper folders for signatures. I felt eyes on me. I couldn't have looked much different from behind compared to when I left. I wasn't shapeless, exactly, but I was wearing slacks and a loose shirt that came down past my elbows. The meds were supposed to be shifting my weight, toward not so much an hourglass as a peanut. I only had the one mirror at home, so I couldn't but guess what I looked like from the rear. I straightened my posture. Pulled in my rear.

While I concentrated on filing, a shuffling exodus took place. "Having a breakfast meeting," said Joy, tapping once on the shelving to get my attention. "Move it or lose it." I had brought a bagel for breakfast; I had planned on eating it on the loading dock, like I usually did. Instead, I retrieved it from my desk and followed behind Mary at the end of the line. A gaggle of women.

The whole department fit around one of the big oval tables in the cafeteria. Joy asked if I wanted to go through the line with the rest of them, since we could charge food eaten at meetings to the department budget, but I was all right with my bagel. Sounds boring, but it was cinnamon and raisin and I mixed honey and butter together to sandwich in between the halves.

I sat with my back to the main cafeteria door. Every so often, during our meeting—conducted around mouthfuls of breakfast burrito, smelling of

Tabasco—Mary, sitting across from me, would glance up and fix someone with a quick smile, disappearing quicker. The last time she did it, I turned around to see who she was smiling at and caught the tail end of an interested stare and raised eyebrow from one of the lab techs as he looked away from me.

Joy's agenda was a short one, just long enough to last through breakfast. It was mundane and pleasantly so. She excused herself afterward to go to a hair appointment. "Gonna swim there?" asked one of the other ladies.

On the way back down the stairs to the office, Mary leaned in close to my shoulder and said: "You always sat down to pee, didn't you?" smiling at herself for having suspected something right, or close to it. She was the closest thing I had to a friend in the department, despite our age difference. We had gone out drinking a couple of times, whenever the stars aligned just right. She had two young kids, a jealous husband, and a personality that wouldn't allow anyone to just sit and watch on karaoke night at The Lariat. The stars didn't align, much.

"Hey, you've lost weight," I said. "You look good." I made it through both sentences without my voice cracking.

"You haven't been gone that long," she grinned.

Long enough for the work to pile up, even with Joy's contribution. I dutifully typed, sorted, filed, and gave myself paper cuts until it was time for lunch and then for several minutes after. Shasta had said she'd meet me for my first day back, Jilly in tow. They had been out of town for a month-and-a-half, visiting distant relatives in other states. "The Single Mom Family Tour" Shasta had called it, undertaken now that Jilly was just old enough to zone out on TV in the car, and plenty cute enough to draw a crowd. I'm sure they both had better things to do than meet up with me for hospital food. It wasn't the first time Shasta had gone out of her way for me in the years since I came out to her. I typed away anxiously, wondering what they would look like, wondering what they would see. Finally, some time after Joy had stopped by to make sure I hadn't missed my break, the front desk paged me overhead. I climbed the stairs to admissions.

Shasta was cross-legged on the floor of the waiting room with Jilly on her lap, nose-to-nose and making faces. Catching sight of me, she stage-whispered: "I want you to meet someone!"

Jilly leaned backward in her mother's arms, forcing Shasta to catch and hold her lest she topple off balance. My little blondie saw me, this me, for the first time upside-down, and laughed for who knows what reason. Shasta tossed her back upright and stood to give me a one-armed hug.

"Jilly, this is your Auntie Lita!"

Jilly gave me a careful once-over, looked away, then back again, right into my eyes. She and I looked as different from each other as Victor and me. I blinked first.

"You look great," Shasta said. It sounded a little practiced, but who was I to fault her for that. Maybe realizing it herself, she followed it up with the real thing: "My god, I can't believe how great you look."

I blushed; I could feel it, deeply. "Hungry?" I asked.

Lunch was on me, deducted from my next paycheck. Shasta made herself a salad of spinach leaves underneath olives and avocado, shredded cheese, sunflower seeds. Jilly wanted a grape juice box and the biggest slice of cheese pizza.

"Isn't that a little much for you?" I said.

Shasta tried something else. "If you don't finish it all, then I get to pick for you next time, okay?"

Jilly thought that was a fine idea. I had a salad, too, but it was mostly lettuce and chicken. Shasta loaded up with dressing before we sat down. I picked us a side of one of the round tables. Me, then Jilly, then Shasta, all in a crescent shape where we had to twist our necks to see each other. Before long, Shasta and I had adjusted our seats so we were kind of three-quarters aimed toward Jilly, and craning every so often to get a bite of food.

"I'm so glad you guys could come by," I said.

"I know. It always feels like forever in between when we see each other," said Shasta. "Why is that?" I shook my head and smiled. Jilly began picking bits of chicken off my salad and distributing them around her pizza, while one bite of crust slowly became mush in her mouth, smack smack smack.

"How's your Mom?" I asked, stirring my plate so the choicest pieces of meat ended up on the edge nearest Jilly.

"She's got a new boyfriend."

"Really?"

"Yeah. Some guy from the coast. Another lawyer. They met at the oncology place in Seattle. He sounds like a nice guy. They go in for the same treatment."

"I've heard breast cancer isn't so uncommon in men," I offered.

"I guess not."

She was sounding happy enough, but she always was good at fooling. She learned early on that the shape of the mouth seems to affect the tone of the words. Pass them through a smile, and they sound all right. Jilly took a big bite of her pizza, after some effort getting it to her mouth, opening wide to get some of the chicken along. She made a face and opened her mouth again, letting the chicken roll off her tongue and onto her lap.

"Come on, baby," said Shasta, smile gone just long enough for the words to get out, then reappearing, more like going along with a joke than really getting into it. Jilly whined, wordless, and squirmed in her seat. "Baby girl, I am counting to three. One, two, three." On three, Jilly went still and sulky. "Say you're sorry," said Shasta.

Jilly said something that sounded like it – two syllables, anyway. Then her little toddler hands set to work replacing the chicken on my plate, carefully piled on one corner of the salad. Shasta rolled her eyes and I smiled.

"He like kids?" I asked. The cafeteria was filling up. A man in a hospital gown slid into a chair opposite us, soon joined by maybe his family.

"He hasn't come visit us yet," said Shasta. She glanced over at the patient with what I thought looked like nervousness. The man was staring at Jilly. He didn't look ill. Maybe just there for an MRI, or something. He smiled. Jilly sang a song about being all finished.

"Here, honey," said Shasta, opening Jilly's juice box for her and handing it over. Jilly took the little plastic straw up between her lips and sucked mightily, stopping once to cough out a bit of purple liquid that had gone down the wrong tube. Shasta sat close, napkin at the ready. She had such a look of concentration on her face I couldn't help myself smiling. She was completely involved in her own life. Absorbed into it, so much that I bet she couldn't even tell that time was passing.

Wanting to be so engaged, I leaned over and kissed Jilly on the top of the head. She went on inhaling her grape juice. The patient was looking at me, now, and Shasta's eyes flicked up. There I went, outside myself, watching time click past.

The table filled. Shasta took a few hurried bites of her salad. She hadn't yet lost all the weight from the pregnancy even now a couple of years on I noticed, kind of ashamed I did.

"Shall we make some room?" I picked up my plate and slid back my chair. That was good enough for Jilly, who slithered down, rolling to her stomach, finding the floor while Shasta cleaned up her place at the table. I reached for Jilly's hand.

"Your daughter is so cute," said one of the patient's family to me.

"Thank you," said Shasta. "I do what I can." The words coming out of smile-shaped lips.

We paused in the lobby long enough for Shasta to kiss me on the cheek. "I'm so proud of you," she said, the weight of Jilly cradled in her left arm pulling the kiss short. She smelled like fabric softener, and took the scent with her out the door. "Say, 'Bye, Auntie Lita.' Bye!"

I took an extra fifteen minutes on my break and spent them in the bathroom, turning my face this way and that, and then touching up my makeup in some way that ended up looking wrong, but I couldn't for the life of me tell you how.

Quitting time came around slowly, and without much more in the way of human contact. I skimmed dictations, made sure they were signed by the providers, slid them into manila folders thick with information. My soundtrack was the soft click of keyboards going at ninety-plus words-per-minute. Usually, after all that hush, I feel the need to clear my mind of everything and either hang on to some silence or pig out on trivial things.

Tonight, I needed the latter. I went to the Safeway deli for dinner and grabbed a gossip magazine while I was there. Back at home, celebrities in candid photographs spread out on my lap, a forkful of dry fried rice at my lips, I remembered that it was family dinner night.

At Mom's insistence, every other Thursday Victor and I were to come home and share some authentic cooking around the old dining room table we had had since I can remember and which Dad had restored some time when I was in grade school. I hadn't been for a couple of months, since the same day I put in at work for my vacation. Mom had made tamales that night; she had insisted, even though the recipe came from Dad's side of the family. Her masa was too dry. Dad put four away, though, no trouble.

Victor and I back in our old places. Mom and Dad at the head and foot of the little oblong table, in the same chairs with different upholstery. Mom was riding Victor pretty hard about Gracie, how she didn't want to interfere, but could he maybe get her to pick a color of hair and stick with it. She didn't have anything against bright, unnatural colors. She just thought a girl who changed things up so much might be trouble down the road. Victor took it well, his terse responses not without levity. There was something else under there in his voice, though, something only a sibling could recognize. He kept Mom in smiles all night, but talking the whole time like he was trying not to get grounded. Same inflection, same vocabulary we'd bring up when we were trying to dodge a lecture as kids.

That's what gave me the courage, when I look back on it. Victor, figuring himself in trouble, keeping Mom happy with thinking about maybe a daughter-in-law, fickle hair and all. When I cut in with: "I've got some news," he gave me that same old grateful look we've passed back-and-forth since before I knew it, excepting when we were both in trouble at the same time.

I think I made sure Mom didn't give a fuck what color Gracie dyed her hair. I tried to tell it so they'd react the same way Victor had when I told him. I spoke slowly, judging how strongly they resisted and changing course in little bits to steer toward the gentlest ending. My story, then, came out one sentence at a time. Dad socked away a fifth tamale. Mom, spotting at one point that I hadn't even finished my first, asked if I was watching my figure.

Dad didn't get it. Victor shed the old grateful expression and got a little embarrassed for me. He had tried to get me to keep it inside around the parents, after I first told him. Not to keep a secret, but to leave it on a need-to-know basis. Like him and his cash flow, he said.

It says more bad about me than him that in the long silence after I reached the period at the end of the last bit of my story I wanted to spill his secret to take the heat back off myself.

Instead, I took a couple more bites of my bone-dry tamale, asked to be excused as polite as I ever had, found my shoes, and let myself out. One big silence inside and outside except for dogs barking down the street.

I didn't even see them the whole rest of the time up to my mini-vacation. Now it was family Thursday again, and Gracie had done such a good job on my hair. I took a quick shower at home to get the tart hospital smell off my skin. Afterward, I dressed in a short-sleeved polo—it made my arms look too thick—

and a pair of jeans. They had a bit more shape than my work pants, squishing my fat around, not quite as forgiving as they had been in the dressing room mirror. I put a pair of nickel studs in my ears and teased my hair so that they were pretty well covered.

I felt confident as I pushed out into the evening air and locked the door behind me. Confidence isn't much different from heat, though, and the vanished sun drew the world's warmth with it over the horizon. With no jacket, I ended up hugging myself halfway along the short walk to Mom and Dad's house.

Then I just stood there, getting just about as cold as possible, reaching a plateau, or the valley floor more like. Victor pulled up in his pretty blue car, a need-to-know purchase, and switched off his headlights.

"Hey," he said, climbing out.

"Hey."

He crunched over the gravel shoulder to stand next to me. "It's gonna be a short one tonight, if you can handle it."

"Got someplace to be?"

He nodded.

"You bring Gracie over, yet?"

"Not yet. You like her?"

"You're mellowing out with her, man."

He grinned and punched me in the shoulder. We turned to face the same way, both staring at Mom and Dad's house.

"What do you think?" I asked.

"I think me and Dad pretty much don't care." It was nice to hear. Dad and Victor were growing more like each other as time went on, which was kind of strange. Something in Victor made Dad a little more youthful, buying himself new power tools without Mom's say-so, and keeping secrets from her like the stash of pot we found in his workshop during my senior year. And just about everything in Dad made Victor quiet, more stoic, but not like a stone, more like a pond.

We stood there for a few more minutes, occasionally seeing a shadow of Mom behind the kitchen curtains. I was definitely on the valley floor now, temperature-wise, with Victor descending toward me. Our paths didn't cross much since he had graduated, except right here.

"I'm gonna go home, I think," I said.

"Want me to say if I've seen you?"

"Nah. But talk to me some time, would you?"

"Yeah. You and Gracie should hang out."

Somehow, he got it in his head to grab me in one arm and pull me into him. He kissed me on the top of the head and muttered something in Spanish I still wish I could remember clear enough to figure out. Then he crunched away, leaving me realizing that he hadn't been anywhere near my cold little valley.

A perverse craving for ice cream snuck up on me. Forget dinner. It was my prerogative, as a grown woman, to skip straight to dessert. In the Dairy Queen drive-thru, it was tough to talk myself down from a large sundae to a small, but my good sense won out. Good sense, and a small, prideful delight that the sugar would go straight to my hips. Before the meds, fat had distributed itself pretty evenly across my torso. Now, my pudge noticeably avoided my waist.

After I got home I could only manage about half of the sundae.

It wasn't much past eight, way too early for bed even at my most side-effect-prone, so I curled up on the couch in an afghan Mom had crocheted for me to take to football games in high school. I tried Shasta on her cell, but she didn't answer. I switched on the TV and zoned out. It's nice to sink beneath myself, once in a while. Just leave behind my concentration, and jagged mess of the day's memories, and not react at all to whatever's on the screen.

At eleven, I hit the off button during the end credits of a cop show. Glancing at the clock, I cursed out loud. A couple solid weeks of it, of being me with my hair and my skin and sort of my body, and I still hadn't solidified the habit of my nightly routine. It took me altogether almost forty-five minutes to take my pills, shower, take off the makeup that hadn't come off by itself, moisturize, and put my hair up. Then another fifteen minutes, which I hardly noticed passing, looking at myself in the mirror, sliding my hands over the portions of my body which stood out of place, playing make-believe with no shame until I realized it. I was built like a rail. Nowhere near enough ice cream.

I checked that my alarm clock was set before sliding between the sheets. The air conditioning kept the room at sixty-seven. I cocooned myself in a comforter, hands down at my sides. As I stepped sideways into dreaming, they alternately felt like a stranger's hands and my own. The last thing I remember from that night was the unshakable feeling that I had a huge responsibility I hadn't been attending to, and that a deadline was fast approaching.

2

It was a few weeks later on a Saturday that Victor set out for Spokane at something like two in the morning. A good chunk of the road lay on reservation land, and tribal police kept pretty regular nine-to-five hours. Once you got into the hills you were pretty much in the clear, smokey-wise. Victor had always liked to speed. Not just to speed but to fling his vehicle around corners, making believe he was drifting sideways in the dust of Pike's Peak. Really, his little Neon gripped the oil-and-gravel fairly well. The one time I had let him drive me into the city I had felt my stomach flung about with the momentum, but not much else.

In the early AM, he drove like a man possessing no real purpose. He was headed to Spokane to meet up with some friends, to catch a hockey game, to bum around and be an unemployed twentysomething.

Deep in the hills, around a curve so tight it moved even his leaden foot to the brake, he saw flames. A car on fire, the orange glow dissected vertically by tree trunks. The smoke dense as the overcast sky. He pulled over, I think pretending that his tires squealed.

Victor always had more of Mom in him than I did, inside and out. A sense of charity for those unknown to him. Black hair, eyes, and mustache. Just like Mom. He got out of his car, felt the mountain air cold in contrast to the sound of cracking fuel, the smell of things burning that shouldn't. "Hey!" he called, once or twice. Crossing the road. Looking both ways, as though it would do any good if another driver like him had come whipping around the bend. Stopping at the first rank of trees to call out, "Is everyone OK?" No accent. He didn't inherit that from Mom.

A shadow of a man—a boy—interposed between the fire and Victor. Others solidified from between the trees. Waiting there or warming themselves there, within reach of the heat but not the light. Cans of Bud in their hands. Victor saw the shape of the blazing car, an old Honda. A couch perched crazily on the hood, bridging over the windshield to the roof. Tongues of flame jabbering stupid, excited.

"Hey, cousin. Want a beer?" called one of the boys. Friendly, drunk.

Victor must have stepped inside the reach of the light. They saw his face, Mom's face. Someone threw their can to the ground and shouted. Feet thudding on pine needles. The boys were all decked out in the red of native pride. Victor didn't have on his colors, but it didn't matter.

He saw four of them, but missed the fifth coming out of the trees to his left with forearm raised like a club. One blow laid him out, and he hit the ground blind. Someone spit on him. Insults landed in English, Salish, and mocking Spanish. Heels and toes landed on his ribs, face, and spine. He had a pistol, but he kept it in the Neon's glove box and sometimes forgot to take it out, even when he let Gracie borrow the car.

Three of the boys picked him up, two under his arms, one at his legs. The other two laughed and went for their beers. Victor knew his blood was running hot, but the hands that gripped him were thick, strong, and tight. No fighting. They hauled him toward the burning car. His skin went hotter than his blood.

"Wanna powwow?" sneered one of the boys.

"Please," said Victor. He hit the hood of the car and rolled half under the couch. His legs dangled off the edge. The shudder of the car's body was enough to slip the couch from its perch. It toppled, its frame splitting down the center line in a burst of sparks, and pinned Victor underneath.

That's where I lose it: the story and my confidence in telling it. I have never been closer to any other man and, as he burned, I slept between flannel sheets.

As I overheated in the bedclothes, and not long after the boys had tossed Victor on like deadfall trimmings, another passerby saw the flaming wreckage. This time the boys scattered instead of offering a beer. Powwow disbanded. The driver flicked his blinkers and left his pickup in the middle of the lane. The small and only blessing of the night was that no one else flew around the hairpin curve while this Samaritan torched his arms pulling Victor out of the blaze. He left some of his blistered skin behind.

This man—who didn't give his name, and who didn't stay in the hospital long enough for me to meet him—had to drive ten miles to get a cell signal, then ten miles back into the middle of nowhere to sit next to Victor while the ambulance and fire trucks made their way through the hills, going maybe three-quarters the speed that Victor had. The EMTs couldn't do much. They called for the med chopper, which put down in a clearing just barely wide enough. The man who had saved Victor rode in the ambulance to get himself treated, pretty well ending his part in the story I'm sure he went on to share a hundred times. I'm stupid and jealous that it's not really mine to tell. Victor, unconscious and unrecognizable, flew in the chopper. Ended up making it to Spokane well ahead of schedule.

I woke up that morning needing to pee like crazy, and knowing next to nothing. I'm pretty sure the two are related. The body takes a primal focus on its needs, and all the higher functions spin, alone, above and unconnected. I sat on the toilet, pushing my penis down at an angle it kind of naturally wanted to resist. Then I took my pills and got in the shower.

Sweat from the night made my skin feel tacky and thick. I slipped my fingers slowly over my arms, my stomach, my sides, my breasts which weren't much but felt fragile and sensitive. The water alone didn't make me feel clean, but the heat at least helped. Looking straight down at myself, the shower hitting the back of my head and sluicing through my long hair, I thought about graduation day several years gone. I had been standing the same way in the shower that day, but with not even these hints of breasts to trick me into feeling womanly, womanish.

I rubbed my eyes, hard water making the corners itch. Another waking come and gone, and my body had again stubbornly refused to go all Kafka on me. No metamorphosis would come for me. I stood trans-fixed as the hot water slowly cooled. Between the thin walls of my building, I could hear the pipes rattle, water rushing to fill the water heater as I drained it dry.

Finally having enough, I stepped out into a haze of steam in my little bathroom. I cursed myself under my breath for not turning on the fan beforehand. A rattle, a whirr, and the air began to clear. A fog-free mirror, I told myself, would be the next of my vain, indulgent purchases.

The past couple of weeks had begun much the same way, in a haze slightly thinner for having the fan running. They ended similarly, a shower to wake up and a shower to go to bed, with nothing much in between. No highs or lows, no rushing up to the peak of the day, descending again to the axis of sleep. The days felt flat, linear. Kind of the way my body appeared in the mirror.

I had started taking pictures of myself with the chintzy little camera on my phone first thing in the morning, after getting ready for work, so I could track my progress. That morning, while Victor lay unidentified in a burn ward, I pursed my lips and took several shots in low-key lighting. No good. I picked the best of the bunch – the one in which I could see a trace of feminine in the curve of my cheek, focusing so intently on that one feature that I didn't notice until later that my eyes in the photo had gone kind of crossed while trying to stare at the lens. The mind is willing, but the body disobeys, rebels.

Worse than that, I thought. The body doesn't even recognize the same language. The body speaks in hormones, in chemical reactions. I can say: soften the lines of my chin. I can make the electrical impulses that form the words that represent the dumb static agony of begging, but the body is deaf.

My flesh spoke in hormones. How frustrating that the hormones seemed able to conjure words, but the reverse was impossible.

The phone buzzed in my hand and Shasta's name came up, replacing the so-so wallpaper image of myself with one of her and Jilly grinning big at Easter time.

"Good morning," I said brightly. Damn the hormones; full speed ahead!

"Hey. Can you come and get her a little early?"

"Sure thing. What's up?" Shasta's mother had treatment at the oncology center in Spokane that day, and Auntie Lita was stepping in to watch Jilly. Shasta wouldn't be back until late that night.

"Mom's feeling pretty crummy, so I figured we ought to give ourselves a bit more time to make the trip."

"No problem. You want me to come over now?"

"Yeah, that'd be good."

I hurried through the rest of my morning routine —keeping it up on the weekends was something of a sticking point for me—and was out the door in five minutes. I drove up to Shasta's mother's house, parking in the driveway, crunching on the gravel. Shasta met me at the front door lugging a car seat.

"Backwards or frontwards?" I asked, accepting it from her in a clumsy little dance.

"She can face front now. Honey, stay inside." Jilly darted for the open door with a laugh, wearing only a diaper, her chubby legs pale and stamping. Shasta caught her around the middle. "Little naked baby! Let's get you some clothes while Auntie Lita gets your seat ready."

My cheapo Camry didn't have any of the fancy buckles or braces that newer models do, so I double- and triple-checked that the seat was fastened securely by the lap belt. When I turned back to the house, Shasta was standing in the doorway, balancing Jilly on her hip. Jilly was wearing pink tights and a polka-dotted tee and pulling on her own ears. I wanted to hug her so hard she split in half, but I settled for teasing her hair. She turned away and buried a sud-denly shy face in her mother's neck.

"Ready for this?" asked Shasta.

"Born ready," I said.

"You look good today."

I shrugged and smiled. "I don't know," I said. I wish I had started, as a child, running tally of how often I would say those three words. I lowered my voice. "It's bad to say it, but I was hoping for more of a change."

Shasta laughed, which started Jilly smiling, which then made Shasta turn her laugh in her daughter's direction, and so on. I joined in. After a bit, we all calmed down. Shasta shook her head. "I can't get over it," she said. "I would kill for your hair, you know?"

I rolled my eyes at her, not without affection. Something more clearly affectionate bubbled up in my throat. "I love you," I said, grinning.

Shasta took it in the tone it was delivered. "I know," she replied, affecting arrogance.

Jilly picked up on it, too. "I love you, Mommy!" she said, only half the syllables as clear as they look on paper. I felt kind of proud that I could understand them. "I know!" crowed Shasta, moving in to bonk noses with our daughter. "I love you, too!" like it was a brand new discovery, outshining anything that came before. For a second, anyway. Shasta looked up at me, her cheek pressed against Jilly's.

"OK, now go with Auntie Lita!" Jilly slithered to the ground and sat, legs sticking out to either side.

"Come on, peanut," came a voice behind us. I turned and saw Shasta's mother, Jeanine, in the hallway, pulling a small overnight bag on wheels behind her.

"Let me get that, Mom." Shasta took the bag and lifted it down the front steps. Jeanine stooped over and lifted Jilly into her arms with a groan.

"You are so heavy! Do you have a kiss for grandma?" Jeanine and I shared a laugh as Jilly smacked her lips, nowhere near managing to plant the kiss. I got the chance to get a good look at Jeanine. Her skin was pale and there was a faint suggestion of hair on her upper lip. Her eyes were dim and clouded, but her mouth slipped into a healthy grin as she demonstrated for Jilly the right way to share kisses with grandma.

"How are you feeling?" I asked, again reaching out a hand to Jilly's curls.

"I'm OK. The treatments make me a little tired. A lot moody."

"I know the feeling," I said. Jeanine gave me a pained, sympathetic smile and set Jilly back down. Shasta returned from the car. "Ready to go, Mom?"

"Always." After one more hug for Jilly, half-acknowledged, Jeanine made her way to the car and climbed into the passenger seat.

"What are you guys going to do with yourselves?" Shasta asked me. Her voice carried a bit of the inflection that she used on Jilly.

"Probably watch some TV, if that's all right."

Jilly jumped flat-footed down the first two steps. "TV!" she laughed. "TV!" Repeating the letters and jumping with both feet down to the bottom step, then turning and hopping up again. TV, TV, then getting her wires crossed somewhere and putting the pause in the wrong place. "VT! VT!" until Shasta cut through, waved bye-bye, got the cold shoulder, and turned to me.

"Call if anything happens."

"Anything at all?"

"You know what I mean."

"Don't worry. If something happens, my parents can help out." That earned me a weird amalgam expression: skepticism and relief combined across her features, smoothing some, creasing and deepening others. I leaned into a hug and finished it off with a boring old: "See you later."

After Shasta and Jeanine disappeared down the road, it was another ten minutes before I got Jilly up in the car and headed out to the park.

I hadn't planned much of a day, figuring we would just take things as they came. My parents didn't know that I had Jilly for the day. If I had told them, we wouldn't have gotten any time to ourselves. Among everything else, I was sure Mom hadn't forgiven me for sinking something of a wedge between her and her granddaughter. It wasn't a wedge made of anything mine.

Jilly was too young to hold a conversation with, even about childish things, but that doesn't mean she kept silent. Where her mother volleyed back and forth with one, two, three, Jilly played a relentless game of verbal cross-country. Endurance chattering. She named everything she saw, tried to repeat anything I said, and sometimes just made noises with her tongue. I tried to keep up, but between chuckling at her antics and not wanting to look like too much of a blabbering idiot in public, I eventually settled back and just listened.

As she spoke her face showed her emotions clearly. She didn't have much experience with scowling, grinning, or whatever it's called when you're being bashful, but I guessed she had a natural talent. Her features were as flexible as clay, but never lost their distinctiveness.

Count me among those who don't really see it when someone says to a mother of her newborn, "Oh, he looks just like his daddy!" or the like. Babies look like babies. Infants look like babies with cuter clothes. Toddlers start to look like themselves, though, and even I can start to pick up on their influences. Jilly had Shasta's eyebrows and maybe a bit of her nose. Her eyes looked paler than either Shasta's or mine. Beneath the chubby cheeks, I thought I could see something of my cheekbones, and the same feminine promise that I had tried to capture that morning with the camera.

We played in the park until lunch time, then went to a local diner for lunch. Jilly let me carry her through the doors and even whined a bit when I set her down in a high chair next to me.

"What would you like for lunch, sweetie?" I asked her.

"Roni!" she clapped. "Tookie?"

"Macaroni and cheese?"

"Tookie." She nodded with finality.

"Cookie after we eat lunch, OK?" I sighed inwardly. You're not supposed to ask the child if your plan is OK. I had read that. Shasta had told me. I just couldn't help myself. People-pleasers don't filter much for the age of the person they're pleasing. Fortunately, Jilly thought it was a reasonable plan and nodded her agreement.

I ordered our food and played a short game of napkin peek-a-boo. After a while, Jilly started squirming and saying, "Tuck."

"Are you stuck?"

"Tuck."

"It's almost time for the food," I said.

Our bowls arrived steaming. Jilly reached her hand out, quick as young Grasshopper. "Careful!" I snatched at her wrist, a fraction of a second too late. Five little fingers squashed into the macaroni. She began to cry almost faster than I would figure the pain could register. "Hot!" I said, pulling out her hand and shaking it loosely to help cool the molten cheese.

"Hot," she repeated through a mess of tears. "Hot." I dipped a paper napkin into my ice water and wiped away the sauce. "Hot," Jilly sniffled.

"No, this is cold."

"Hot." She reached for my water glass with her free hand.

"No. Cold."

My phone rang. Immediately I could feel excuses spin up to speed in my head, expecting Shasta to be on the other end. My voicemail would pick up in four rings; I shoved Jilly's bowl out of her reach and raced to answer. I didn't register that the incoming number was unfamiliar until I had already said: "Hello?"

"May I speak with Lita?" came a girl's light voice.

"Speaking."

"Is Victor Hernandez related to you?"

The surface of my skin went cold, the deeper layers hummed with raw heat. I choked on nothing and gulped down more. Jilly went silent, except for a sweet: "All done." The police found Victor's phone in his car. He liked buying them off-contract, discarding numbers, trading up every few months. Mine was the only number he had listed in his contacts. The girl on the other end of the line asked me little details, building a bed of clinical detachment. She said where she was from. She mentioned that Victor was in critical condition, then clarified that the word has a specific medical definition. She asked if he was allergic to any painkillers, or was I aware. I mostly had no answers.

"Does Victor have a living will or durable power of attorney?"

"I'm his lawyer," I blurted. Such a slight lie, with so little behind it. Graciously, I don't think the nurse, or whoever she was, believed me and we moved on.

"Are you in the area?"

"I can get there."

"Does he have any other family you would like me to notify?"

This girl—maybe just out of nursing school, maybe still in school and getting all the crap duties—spoke with such gentleness, such openness that I pictured all her words double-spaced. Plenty of room to read between, to add marginalia. I didn't have anything to add.

I rattled off Mom and Dad's number, the same number we had had since I was young. We said goodbye. Immediately, I tried calling Shasta. No answer. The second call went straight to voicemail. Not a whole lot of cell coverage on the wide road to Spokane.

Steam curled up off the dish of macaroni. Smoke from a fire near death.

"Do you want to go for a car ride, little girl?"

I had to stop for gas on the way out of town. While Jilly counted to five, over and over, I bought her a sleeve of Oreos.

3

We managed an hour in the car before Jilly's first tantrum. It happened as we were coming down the pass. She had stayed fairly quiet, munching her cookies. I kept glancing in the rearview mirror to check on her. Once, she grinned back at me, displaying a row of chocolate-black teeth. And me, like a good parent, without even a travel bottle of Scope in the car.

As we came around the last tight mountain curve, though, we slowed with the traffic and passed by Victor's car on the shoulder. Flares and police tape cordoned off a wedge of the lane, and a flagger in a bright green vest directed Eastbound and Westbound through the bottleneck. A deputy's cruiser had angled itself in front of the Neon, its lights going.

I felt strangely as though I ought to stop, get out, and tell the deputy or whoever would listen that I was

Victor Hernandez's sister, that I knew things and was a part of this.

The change in speed, the gradual crawl to a halt as we waited for the flagger must have been unacceptable to Jilly. She began to sob, then stretched out toward me and said: "Hep."

"We're not there yet, baby," I said.

"Hep!"

"We'll get moving again here quick."

A semi carrying a load of logs rumbled past, the last in the line of traffic coming our way. The flagger spoke into his walkie-talkie, then spun his sign around and beckoned us forward. We inched past, the line not picking up speed until the wreck was too far behind for a rubber neck to keep in view. I felt my fingers turn icy and I kept my eyes on the road, turning the wheel as gently as possible.

The afternoon sun sliced through the forest. We picked up speed, my tendency toward obeying the speed limit placing me eventually at the rear of the pack. Before long, Jilly and I were alone on the road. Shadows cut the asphalt into a thousand pieces; passing over and through them was like driving through a golden strobe light. I bent the rearview mirror down so I could see Jilly's face. She had it all scrunched up, turned away from the window. Her skin went pink, blue, pink, blue as the trees flickered past.

"Is it too bright, sweetie?"

"Sop," she said.

"I didn't bring a hat for you." I tried to think of how to shield her from the sun. I had the emergency kit that Dad had given me one Christmas. There was a fire blanket in it, but I kind of worried that if I used it as a window shade I'd forget to pack it back up. And then where would it be in a real emergency. Buried under the garbage on the floor.

"Sop," said Jilly. "Hep."

"It's time for night-nights," I hazarded. No dice. I slowed down, but even at forty-five the sunlight toggled like there was a toddler at the switch. A trembly little crescendo came into Jilly's voice.

There's something deep, hot, and solid about the sound of a child crying. It's the first language we learn, and we never forget it, though we layer words and words overtop. It's unfit for dialogue, pouring only out. The only response it can accommodate is silence, drowning out everything else and storing its own kind of momentum so that even when silence is the right response you might not realize it as the scream goes on and on. I lasted maybe five minutes—though I'm pretty sure time dilated for me a hair.

I pulled over, left the engine running, and climbed into the back seat next to Jilly. I sat there, dumbly patting her on the head while she tore at her shoulder harnesses. The scream went from a forlorn cry for help to an angry wail. I tried to get her to take a drink of water, but she flung the sippy cup to the floor. Pawing after it, I found a roll of thick blue shop towels. Another gift from Dad.

I rolled down the rear window on the sunny side of the car and tore off a strip of the towels. They were thick enough, opaque enough to filter the sun to a dark, watery blue. It took both hands and an elbow to hold four strips of them in place and get the window rolled up, pinching them tight. The inertia of Jilly's meltdown bled out slowly as I fashioned the same kind of shade on the other side of the car.

By the time I got back behind the wheel, she was down to a case of the sniffles. "Thirsty," she said. I twisted around and retrieved her cup, which she popped in her mouth as if she had been parched for hours.

We pulled back out into the road. My makeshift sun screens dampened the harsh cuts of light and, as a glance in the rearview mirror confirmed, Jilly seemed much more content.

After a couple dozen miles or so, we passed below the tree line. My cell phone buzzed in my purse. I waited until I was on a straightaway to fumble for it, flick it on, check the message. I had missed a call while out of service on the pass. My thumb plugged in my voicemail password by feel.

"Hey, it's me." Shasta's voice. "What are you doing? Call me."

"Mama," said Jilly.

"Yeah, just a sec, honey." I pulled over at my next chance, the dirt entrance to a private ranch. Rusted cars littered what looked like an old alfalfa field. An RV, missing its wheels, was up to its windshield in weeds. I had a couple of bars of signal. A small line of pickups sped past, going my way; I waited until distance had muffled their engines, then I dialed Shasta's number.

"Hey," she answered. "How's my girl?"

"OK. Listen, we're in the car, on our way to Spokane."

"What?" A burst of static either drowned out the rest of what she said or just filled the silence.

"Are you driving?" I asked.

"Yeah, hold on—" After a couple of seconds and another whoosh of white noise, Jeanine's voice came on the line. "Hello?"

"Hi. Jilly and I are on our way over." It sounded to me like the windows were down in their car.

"To Spokane?" Jeanine was almost shouting. "I can't turn off the speaker—how do you do this, sweetie—"

Two low beeps and the call disconnected. I waited for a quick count to fifteen, then tried dialing again. No answer.

"Mom, Mom," Jilly said, carefully pronouncing the last M. I got back into the driver's seat and turned to face her.

"We'll see her soon, missy girl," I said with a smile. It was kind of a lie, and I don't know if I sold it. At what age did I start to pick up on things like that? All I could remember at the time was being seven years old, in grade school, and feeling pretty darn sure I was smarter than all the teachers, and easily more clever than the principal who wore stupid hats on assembly days and sang off-key.

Before pulling back out onto the highway, I texted Shasta a couple of lines. *Driving to Spokane. Jilly is fine.* I paused with my thumbs lightly resting on the phone's keyboard before settling on: *Something happened to Victor. He's in the hospital there.*

Something happened. Not really good enough. I wanted to pour a bucket of fear, loss, and helplessness into those words, but they were small, just a few pixels wide. No crescendos in that weak language, no dynamic range, no rebel yell or whimper that doesn't first pass through gate after gate of logic and interpretation. I waited until my phone confirmed the message had been sent, then hit my blinker and pulled back onto the empty pavement.

The speedometer topped the limit and climbed another five miles-per-hour before my instinct won out over my anxiety. More than once I thought I felt my phone vibrating with a message, but each time I checked, the mailbox was empty. After a while, the hypnosis of the road set in. We left the trees behind and, tipping down the rearview mirror for a glance, I saw that Jilly had fallen asleep. Her head craned forward, putting her neck at what I thought must have been ninety degrees. A story came to mind of a girl who choked to death like that on a family vacation, while her parents thought she was just enjoying a long snooze. I couldn't remember where I had read it, though. More than a few opportunities to pull over came and went while I ferreted through my memory, vaguely suspicious that the story was an urban legend.

A slow little gnawing just behind my navel grew. I pulled over to the shoulder, braking too lightly and spitting gravel with a drawn-out growl. Before I could turn the engine off, Jilly made a soft hoot, which sounded to me like a violent roar but a long way off. Not strangled, then. I checked the clock. It had been a while since her last diaper change, but I couldn't pinpoint how long exactly.

"Can you hold on, baby?" I asked quietly. I lifted my foot off the brake and, ever so gently, crept back into my lane.

Not even a minute later, I heard a cough from the backseat and Jilly said: "Hep."

"No, Jilly. It's time to sleep." The next sound I heard was guttural and hot and brought on its heels a stench of bile that, given my superhuman sense, made me gag and taste acid. I let off the gas and tilted back the mirror. Jilly's chin and shirt were covered in black vomit— blood, I convinced myself without hesitation. Oreo, came a cooler thought. The shoulder there wasn't hardly wide enough for a compact, but I swung into it anyway and hit the blinkers. "Oh, baby, I'm sorry," I said in the tone of a hum, repeating myself while I wound down all four windows dislodging the sun shades in the process. The close air was heavy with chocolate and sick.

I tore through my purse, looking for tissues. Finding none—even though I could have sworn I packed a travel pouch full of them—I remembered the shop towels. I popped my door and went around to the back, opposite the road. My makeshift curtain fluttered lightly in the breeze. Climbing in next to Jilly I saw huge, undigested fragments of cookie. They must have scraped like hell coming up. Going down, too, for that matter. I should have been paying closer attention.

"Hep," she said, her big eyes buoyed on tears.

"Take a drink." I held her cup up to her lips so she could get a little water. She only took a sip before shaking her head and pushing the cup away. I tore off a handful of towels.

The puke had soaked into her clothes, the cover on the car seat, the foam. Sopping up the mess, I kept folding and refolding the towel, trying to get the most out of each square inch. Even so, it took two, three, four more handfuls before I was satisfied the worst of the slop was gone. Jilly made a gagging noise partway through the job and I rushed to hold a clean-ish wad in front of her face. False alarm.

Finally, I got up the nerve to unbuckle and lift her out. Her clothes were slimy and ice-cold, and a brownish pool had formed beneath her. Her feet were the least messy, so I convinced her to stand while I stripped off her clothes and diaper. One last swipe with a clean towel and she was good to go.

"Sit here for a sec, OK?" I piled the stuff on the floor into sort of a nest and let her crawl down into it. She grinned up at me, pieces of Oreo caught between her teeth.

I leaned my head out into the clean air and took a deep breath, then dove back into the task. The roll was nearly empty when I finished soaking up, spreading around, and generally being ineffective toward the mess. "Hep," said Jilly. She had stayed where I had put her, sure, but she had managed to find a bottle of 10W-30 and was industriously working at the cap.

"No, honey. Can you give that to me?" Nothing. "Give that to me." I reached for it and earned a yelp of protest. She tugged it out of reach. "God damn it!" I stretched and yanked the bottle from her hands, tossing it up into the front seat. Jilly screamed. I sat back, right onto a cold spot. I raised my hands to cover my face, all sorry and suddenly scared to show her my mutable expressions. The stench on my fingers wormed down my throat and I only barely got my head turned before I started retching.

"I'm sorry, Jilly," I gasped in between heaves. Tears streamed from my eyes; my stomach clenched. I managed to get down on all fours just outside the door and let my body give up.

The heaves went dry after four or five of them. My eyes cleared and brought the ground into a strange, tight focus. My fingers, splayed, dirty, bracketing a sprout of thistle. My nails, hopelessly caked with grime.

A U-haul truck came dopplering by, its engine fading behind the whoosh of air drawn in its wake. I took a shaky breath, then a stronger one. The heaviest scent was of sagebrush.

"Are you OK?" I turned my head to fix on Jilly.

"Boff," she said. Then a sentence full of words I couldn't make out. I nodded and smiled and wiped my lips on the back of my hand, timed to an exhale. Whatever had upset her stomach didn't seem to be weighing her down anymore. Nothing more than a bad diet, I figured. My muscles had all gone weak, and my bones felt as if they were made of thawing ice, but the deep down guts of me felt all right.

"Time for a diaper," I said. Jilly struggled to climb out of her nest, but I pressed her back into it. "Stay there for just a second, sweetie." When I pulled away my hand she started to claw her way up again. I narrowed my eyes, which made her giggle and freeze. "Red light," I said. Then: "Green light," with a big smile. Her eyes sparkled; her laughter a little more so. I took a step backward.

"Red light," I sang. Another step. Jilly, frozen, squeaked. I kept her in view through the rear window as I moved to open the trunk. Her head tilted up and back, like a salamander about to scent the air. "Red light," I repeated. I popped the trunk. The old hinges squeaked as the door swung up, obscuring Jilly from me. "Red light." I hung on to the first syllable.

The inside of my trunk was a mess. On the many lists I have kept in my life, the entry for cleaning the car has always gravitated bottom-wards. "Diapers, diapers." The benefit being that nothing gets lost, even if it does get forgotten. I uncovered a half-full bag of disposable diapers, a size one down from what Jilly currently wore. They would do fine. I turned up an economy-sized bottle of mouthwash, too, still factory sealed. I wouldn't go so far as to say someone was looking out for me, but I'll allow that maybe God's sense of pity was on the rise.

It took both hands to slam the trunk with enough force to catch. After it stuck, I noticed two little legs sticking out horizontally from the open rear door. "Jilly!" She shrieked, launched her naked self, and hit the gravel butt first. I rushed to help her up, to dust her off, ready for tears. But she must have been seeing green. Not even caring, not even noticing how sharp the ground was underfoot and on tender skin, she ran in her knees-locked way around the front of the car.

For a moment, I just stared. Naked as a jaybird, she screeched some sort of freedom call and crossed the white line. My motherly instincts finally kicked in. I dropped the diapers and took off after her, not calling out in case it would speed her on. Not a car in sight, not an engine within earshot, but my ears burned hot knowing I would keep this a secret from Shasta.

I caught her up. She didn't get far. Better luck next time.

"Green light," she wailed. Then, "Red red red!"

She fought every step, bursting arms and legs out from her core. I retrieved the diapers with one hand and got her laid out on the back cushions, wedged in against the armrests of her car seat. Imagine a dying fish, oxygen starved. Now give it four appendages and one immortal scream. A stretch of profanities whizzed through my mind, ear to ear, as I turned her, flattened her, tore the diaper, lost the tabs, laid her flat again, snagged her ankles in a death grip, and finally stuck the whole writhing mess back into the booster and snapped the harnesses together.

"There!" I crowed. Then, softer, "All done." Jilly fell into a coughing fit and gradually calmed.

She was still naked, except for the diaper. The stench of stomach acid clung to the upholstery, my skin, and the air itself. My roll of shop towels was pretty much gone. We were still an hour out from the hospital. Two hours on from home.

Just for a second, I rested my cheek on Jilly's bare legs. They were cool and soft and smelled all right, given the circumstances. Then she kicked me off.

I gathered up the litter which had fallen from the car and slipped it into the trunk. I closed up the doors I had opened for ventilation and got back behind the wheel. As I started back onto the road, I had both front windows rolled down, but as we picked up speed the noise of wind and the buffeting got to be too much.

A relative silence cradled us. There beyond the trees, the sun was a steady flow of warmth. I cranked open the vents, the thermostat turned a bit into the red so that Jilly wouldn't get too cold.

The road droned on beneath our tires. Jilly fell asleep without a warning, head lolling back. I gazed at her features. She didn't look a thing like her mother, in that moment which, of course, made me think of her mother.

◆ ◆ ◆

On our graduation day, Shasta wore a pale yellow strapless sundress and cork-brown wedges. I wore my hair down and picked a pair of silver earrings that stayed mostly hidden. Even so, Mom asked before I left the house why could I not take anything seriously. I met up with Shasta in the hallway outside the gym. Teachers prowled up and down, clipboards in hand, distributing caps and gowns and checking off names.

The boys got black gowns; the girls got red. The physics teacher handed us our packages. Mine had my given name scribbled on the lid in blue ballpoint. The contents were black. Not a big surprise, but I had spoken with the vice-principal a couple weeks before and he had been all kinds of supportive. He used to be the guidance counselor. After meeting with him and explaining things beyond what he had gathered from gossip, I figured that I would get a red gown, and also that maybe I could be president someday.

Shasta watched me opening the package. Hers was still closed.

"Here," she said, handing over the box.

"No, it's OK. No big deal."

"It's the biggest fucking deal of the day." Serve, volley, score. She almost never swore. Blushing on her behalf, I took her package and opened it. I tried on the crimson cap; it felt lopsided on my hair. Shasta adjusted it, frowned, then returned it to where it had started.

"Yep," she said. I smiled, probably the most genuine smile I had had in years. I offered her the box with my old name. "No, thanks," she said. "I'll go yellow." She grinned and took only the cap and tassel.

We walked together, Pomp and Circumstance playing dreadfully slow. She in her sundress, me in red, shuffling forward on a wave of whispers. In the bleachers where we sat through the commencement, she stuck out like a sore thumb. I don't remember anyone minding.

After the ceremony, Mom wanted pictures with everyone. I've got one of the prints in my wallet, still. In it, Jeanine is holding tiny Jilly in one arm and hugging Shasta with the other. Dad and Victor stare at the camera with matching lazy smiles. I'm bumped up against Shasta, and Mom against me. A good third of the frame is empty, because Mom misjudged the distance to the lens and kept urging us all to scoot in.

Later that day, as we said our goodbyes, I gave Shasta a crushing hug and told her: "I love you." She said the same back. I've heard people and songs complain that those three words mean too little in this day and age, but I think they mean too much, too many things. Not that I have any alternatives to propose.

◆   ◆   ◆

I heard Jilly click her tongue in the backseat, and sneeze. Then I felt her hand on the back of my neck. Startled, I turned my head. "How did you reach—" She was unbuckled, standing on her seat, leaning forward, braced against my headrest. I tried to override my urge to stamp on the brakes and only caught it about halfway. The car jerked and Jilly fell forward, unable to catch herself. Her head rebounded off the passenger seat and I lost sight of her as I tried to steer safely to the shoulder.

She began to wail. I threw the car into park as soon as I could, then leapt from my seat without turning off the engine. Jilly's howl descended from a clear siren to a phlegm-clogged yowl. She had landed face-down in the gap between seats. I pulled her up by the shoulders, murmuring soft words, staring into her watery eyes. She looked okay. She looked okay, but her scream was of one betrayed. My fingertips tingled, as if waking. She wouldn't stop. I tried to soothe her. She pushed me away and wouldn't stop.

I hit the window with an open palm and let out my own too-deep howl. There was a word in there, at least to start with, but it got lost in the harmony.

4

When we arrived at the hospital in Spokane, Victor was unconscious, his room shut tight. Shasta was still occupied getting her Mom set up in the Oncology ward. My parents were on the road. Gracie, Victor's hairdresser girlfriend, had left me a message asking for more details. All of us separated by time and activity, but at least I could communicate again. I called Gracie back and explained what little I knew. She was sorry, so sorry. At the end of our brief conversation, she asked me to let her know if there was anything she could do for me, and I said: "Likewise."

I'm sure I looked homeless and pitiable, roaming the halls with half-naked Jilly in my arms. She was sleepy, content to rest her head on my shoulder unless I stopped moving. Every so often I passed by Victor's room. Its door remained shut and the space behind it was silent. The nurse's station was right close by. I traded polite smiles with the clerks on duty on each revolution.

Shasta texted to say she was at the main entrance and to come by with Jilly. Jilly brightened up as soon as she saw her Mom. I couldn't say I was sorry enough times as I handed over our half-naked toddler, sending with her a wafting of leftover puke. Shasta just smiled and shook her head at my apologies, deflecting them. Her hair looked limp, and the impression carried over to the rest of her.

"Are you guys going back?" I asked.

"I got us a room for the night."

"Oh. Can I help you pay?"

One, two, three, and her last little shake of the head ended it, divided us into a new round. "Are you going to be all right?"

I shrugged. "My parents will be along in a bit. He still hasn't woken up yet."

Shasta shifted Jilly's weight. "OK. OK, I think we're going to go to the hotel. Call if you need anything, though."

"Thanks. Bye, sweetie," I said, waving at Jilly.

"Bye bye, Eeta," she said in four bright tones.

I stood alone in the waiting room for a few minutes, gaze unfocused. A special kind of silence filled me up, the silence of other people's lives going on around mine without intersection. It was getting dark outside and I became gradually aware that I was studying my imperfect reflection in a bank of double-paned windows. It was like being in a fun house, but not knowing if the tweaked angle or bend of the surface was intended to make me look my best or most monstrous.

My phone was free of messages. I roamed back toward Victor's room. The halls were bright and wide, but I still hugged the wall, trying to stay out of the way of anyone who looked like they belonged.

The ward clerk caught my eye. "You don't have to wait outside if you don't want to."

"Thanks," I said. She smiled and bent over her paperwork. Now I felt almost obligated to go in, to sit in the dark beside his bed, to see him wrapped in bandages like an invisible man. "Thanks."

There's a point, I think, at which imagination and memory are pretty much indistinguishable. The further into the past you trace the more they commingle and become fused. The future, though, is strangely clear, a thing of imagination only. A dimension of a single quality unfelt. The difference between the expectation of the needle and the wound of the puncture.

I stood there on the tip of the needle, tracing the artificial wood grain of Victor's door, unsure of which

direction to fall. Come on memory; invalidate my
fantasy.

The brushed-nickel handle was cold and smooth.
The door, swinging inward, took more of my weight
to get moving than I had expected. The result was an
awkward step-shuffle which nobody saw. The lights
were off in Victor's room, but the Venetian blinds
were angled open allowing in the halogen-white glow
of the streetlights just outside. His body was indis-
tinct, draped in white cloth so that he looked to me
like sand dunes on a beach. The hissing, hushing of
the respirator was the sound of the waves. We had
taken a family vacation to Hawaii once, back in
middle school, after fire season had ended and Dad
had some time off. I remember snorkeling and tag-
ging along with Mom to one of the many little bou-
tiques because she hadn't packed a bathing suit she
liked. I remember trying on a bikini in the dressing
room while Mom was busy hounding the staff.

Victor had disappeared from our hotel one night,
and Dad got so angry I thought maybe the spirit of
the volcano had stolen into him, human sacrifice the
only way to calm him down. I wasn't volunteering. I
said I'd search the beach while Mom and Dad went
out in their rental car, but as soon as they were gone
I slunk back inside and stole a tiny swig of Jim Beam
from the mini bar.

Victor made it back before Mom and Dad. He had been with a girl he met in the courtyard. I don't remember what Dad did when they returned from their search, but I can vividly recall the silent anger on Victor's face the day we left as he took the blame for the bill for my sip of whiskey.

Not much of his skin was visible, but what little I saw around his eyes and lips was misshapen and dark. Every one of his muscles seemed paralyzed, the only motion coming from the mechanical rise and fall of his diaphragm.

I looked at the foot of his bed for a chart, but this hospital had gone electronic. No bits of data left loose for those curious or in need of distraction. A whiteboard on the wall showed that Becky was the RN, and Norene was the CNA. A monster of a TV perched on a metal shelf above the bathroom door, old metal dials on the front making me think maybe it had been picked up cheap in a yard sale. The wallpaper gave me the same impression.

Two chairs and a folding cot had been set in one corner. I pulled one of the chairs over to Victor's bedside and sat down. For a few minutes, nothing changed. Not even my thoughts had much motion. Tears came to my lids, then took their sweet time, refusing to spill over, feeling like nothing so much as a sneeze that just won't come. Victor's hands were bandaged like mittens, flat down at his sides. I wanted to hold one. My thoughts slowed so much they went back in time, all the way back to the night of Shasta's party.

I had gone home in the pre-dawn cool, gray light seeming to brush my skin like a sweet breath. I had unloaded a weight, or at least had shared some of the lifting. The lights were all off in the house, and as I let myself in the front door I could smell the stale scent of a full night's sleep.

As I tiptoed into the kitchen for a glass of water, Victor's voice had come out of the gloom. "Dad was up until three waiting for you." My heart leapt, startled, and refused to come down.

"You got home early, then." I twisted on the kitchen faucet a fraction.

Victor strolled in from the living room, wearing his PJs. I could still smell cigarette smoke on him. "I got my lecture already," he said.

I filled up a glass and took a big swallow of luke-warm water. "And?"

"Grounded." He shrugged. He held a mug loosely in one hand, then tilted it toward me. I filled it up for him from the now-cool tap. "You're gonna get worse."

"We were just up talking," I said, rote lying.

"Whatever." He took a sip of water, swirled it around in his mouth, then spat it cleanly into the sink next to me. "Awful lot of talking."

I had a moment, there, where telling him everything would have been as easy as opening my mouth.
The words were already there, piled up behind my
lips. A featherweight momentum could have carried
them out. Instead I took a drink, noted the grease of
lipstick—hers or mine—on the rim of my glass, and
turned away.

"You wouldn't understand."

He had chuckled, snorted, whatever.

In his hospital room, carrying nothing inside of
me but hot courses of regret, I knew he would have
understood. We passed our childhoods like ships at
harbor, moored together at night, by day navigating
different seas entirely. He knew somehow every inch
of me and when I did finally come out to him it was
as if he had already known. That night, in the kitchen,
maybe he already did.

"I'm sorry," I said to his bound-up face. Still
couldn't quite get the tears to flow, but an errant speck
of dust did at least startle a sneeze out of me.

Two sharp knocks at the door, and then Mom
strode right in, Dad behind her with his hands in his
jeans pockets.

"Get the lights, hon," said Mom. "Oh, sweetheart."
Her voice dipped as the harsh fluorescents blinked
on. She came to stand at Victor's side opposite me.
For a moment, we all looked at the blinding white
bandages. Then Dad said: "Hey, kiddo," to me.

"Hi." The respirator hissed and I thought for a moment I caught that old-memory smell of Victor's high school cigarettes. "I haven't seen the doctor yet," I offered. Nothing. I backed out of my seat and stood up. "You want a seat, Dad?" He shook his head. We all stood around, dumbly still, our breaths gradually falling into sync with the rhythm of the respirator.

"Look at all this," Mom said. "We can't afford this."

"It's fine," Dad replied, not taking his eyes off where his son's dark throat disappeared beneath the gauze.

"Don't tell me it's fine." It was a trademarked mother mutter, plenty loud to hear, quiet enough to claim she was talking to herself.

"I'm going to get a cup of coffee," I said. "Let me know if the doctor comes by?"

Mom nodded absently. Dad said: "Yeah." As I slipped out the door, I heard Dad's voice again. "Be OK, son."

The cafeteria was half-full, but the diners were scattered in ones and twos around a collection of tables sized for families. The air was far from still, with clinking silverware and the hollow chock of heavy ceramic mugs against Formica. No conversation, or none pitched so it could be overheard.

A girl younger than me stood behind a cash register. "A cup of coffee, please," I said.

"It's free."

I smiled to thank her, got a bit of a smile back as change. I filled a styrofoam cup from the push-button dispenser nearby then found myself a seat alone at a table for four.

Be OK.

Dad had a lot of experience with that sentiment, fire and rescue having been a major part of his life since he was old enough to volunteer. He lived with his scanner on, the patterns of tones familiar to our whole family. We could sleep through a fire call, and wouldn't miss a second of dialogue if a car crash interrupted one of our shows. Victor's accident had been outside his jurisdiction, otherwise I'm sure he would have been first on scene.

When I was in grade school, he got a call I wish I could remember better.

As soon as the police forwarded the call, Dad and his buddies put together a search party. A mother says her baby is missing, so we go find that baby, that was the reasoning. It took them only an hour or so to find the kid, whose name doesn't come to mind. His mother took him and moved out of town not much after all this.

The kid had found a storm drain down the street from his house and wriggled in through the gap where the grille joined to the curb. Erosion and the city's cheap concrete had made a pocket just right to explore under the sidewalk. When the search party converged, it was Dad's buddy Uncle Scott who took on the job coordinating. He had a baby girl back home, not much older than the missing kid.

They tried just reaching in and pulling on the kid's legs, but he was wedged in good. Plus he kicked at his rescuers like a billy goat, making it hard to get a solid hold on him. Dad managed to get both ankles in his grip, but even the slightest tug made the kid wail, a shriek that drove right to the core of each dad and mom within earshot. They found out later that a bent-off chunk of rebar had caught right under the kid's ribcage, so that when Dad pulled it kind of hooked under the bone with I imagine a sick relentless pressure.

That was after two hours on the scene. Then it started to rain. Not an April drizzle, but a sky-sweeping burst of thick, heavy, dirty drops. The kid's head was angled down in the path of the drainage.

Uncle Scott called in everyone he could and even press-ganged some rubberneckers to sandbag the area, to divert the gutters so they flowed across the street. Dad led up that team. I remember his fingernails the next day, cracked and grimy. While they built makeshift dams and channels, Uncle Scott and one of the paramedics kept up trying to free the kid. They removed the grille and knocked out enough of the asphalt around the drain so they could almost get down to the kid's level, but all it really gave them was more room to maneuver. They still couldn't reach him, couldn't move him, and couldn't shut him up. The thickened sky brought night on too soon.

Through all this, Uncle Scott had done his best to keep the Mom at a distance. She did all right for the first couple of hours, but she lost it when the clouds burst. She broke free of whichever friends or family had been with her and launched herself right into Uncle Scott. Her voice pitched all over the place, a hopeless little boat in a big angry sea, up and down on waves. Her son heard her, and no doubt made some noise himself, trapped, scared, and buried. I would have broken, and I mean snapped clean in half. I would have done nothing to calm the storm. I can put myself there, in the middle of that panic and thudding heartbeat moment, and I can see myself fail everyone.

Uncle Scott just took it. He glanced at Dad; their eyes met for an instant. Then he took the kid's mom aside and let her cry and let her offer suggestions and let her pulse slow down against his while Dad picked up the slack and kept as much water as possible out of the drain system.

They outlasted the storm, but it took survival of six more hours before they finally got the kid free. Ended up jackhammering the next slab of sidewalk over and digging in, patiently, from the side. Sometimes Uncle Scott did the digging, sometimes he was down there with the kid, arms up to his shoulders in the eroded hole, checking a brace on the rotten concrete and muttering good thoughts so the kid could hear, if he was even still awake.

Three in the morning, they got him free. Their excavation made enough room to maneuver, freeing him from the iron rebar hook, scraping him something awful against the rough cement, but finally pulling him out into fresh air and warm hands.

The mother cried and cried as if she had been apart from her son forever, instead of just a few feet away and separated by six inches of poorly man-made rock. Uncle Scott had big hands that swallowed the mom's when he gave them a final shake and sent them off to the safety and reassurance of the hospital.

That night, or morning I guess, Dad put an arm around Uncle Scott's shoulder and asked, "Are you gonna be OK?" Probably a nod or a grunt was what he got back. Good enough. Dad came home and slept until almost noon, getting up once at nine to yell at me for having my cartoons on too loud.

After that night, Uncle Scott came by to visit more often, all beered up. I saw him cry one of those times, sitting on the couch with Dad, fingers up over his eyes to hide the tears but deep red wrinkles cutting out into view and stretching into his crew cut. His wife left him for her own sake.

Then one Sunday morning in July, Dad got a phone call he didn't talk much on. He left the house in a hurry. Game shows on the TV playing to an empty room. He came back at lunch time to tell us that Uncle Scott had passed on, catching us kids one after the other with the news instead of rounding us up like for an announcement. Then he took Mom and left us home alone. Victor went out to the back porch to smoke a stolen cigarette. I took one of Mom's Mary Kay mailers into the bathroom and played make believe with all the colors.

Uncle Scott had been enough of a churchgoing guy that the memorial at Our Lady of the Valley drew a good crowd—all of his fellow parishioners plus everyone associated with fire and rescue. The place was packed, but it emptied out fast. Tables full of Safeway cookies and coffee snagged us hangers-on. Mom held onto Dad with one hand, a styrofoam cup in the other from which they shared sips. I sat on a metal folding chair and nibbled the edges of a crispy macaroon, listening to everyone.

Among the talk of relatives taking the chance to catch up on each others' lives, I caught strings of two conversations from different ends of the room.

"Outta nowhere," said a woman to my left.

"I remember that Fourth of July, two, three years back," said a man to my right.

"Must have been fighting it for a long time. I've got a cousin with the bipolar thing. It's pretty rough on her family. Just didn't think Scottie had that kind of trouble, you know?"

"You remember? Worst was that house with all the junk in it. The packrat."

"He hid it pretty well until Cora left."

"Scott said there was something toxic in the baby's room. Toys from China or something. Wasn't much hope."

"I didn't see her today. Did she come?"

"Or I think it was twins. Anyway. Didn't make it. Made me mad, you know? On the way back to the station, Scott told me to let it go. Just like that. Just let it go. I dunno."

"I kind of hoped she wouldn't, but I kinda hoped she would."

I wanted to get up and grab the hands of the woman and the man and tug them together and say: "Talk to each other." It was an impulse I didn't completely understand then, but I think I do now. They were each trying to get at the same conclusion from different directions. In my scrambled brain, too young to get the concept of depression or to realize I was on my own collision course with the stuff, I felt as if I were listening to two kids in class trying to work the same math problem without success. I didn't know the answer either, but I sure as hell wanted to find out what it was, if for no other reason than to put my curiosity to sleep.

I sipped at my coffee. Be OK. Uncle Scott reached out and took hold of the kid's damp, cold ankle and could feel a pulse. Dad laid a hand on the foot of Victor's bed and listened to the respirator and the IV pump.

The coffee left a bitter lump in my throat. I went back to Victor's room.

"Any word?" I asked.

"A nurse came in," Mom replied. "The doctors will be around first thing in the morning."

I nodded. "I guess I'll go find a place to sleep. You guys OK?"

"We're fine."

As I turned to leave, Dad's voice found me gently. "Goodnight, Lita."

◆　◆　◆

Shasta answered on the first ring. "Hello?"

"Can I stay with you tonight?"

Her motel wasn't far. Walking distance. I felt underdressed for both the weather and the big city, but Shasta answered the door in her pajamas and I felt OK. She gave me a long hug. Jilly lay curled like a shrimp in the middle of the room's queen bed. I collapsed on one side of her. Shasta took the other after switching out the lights.

More than once, if my drowsy memory can be trusted, I woke to Shasta's fingers soothing my shoulder and cheek.

Part Two: A Disease You Can Believe In

5

Mirror-me looked up and down. To get her in full view, stem to stern, I had to stand across the room from my vanity. The distance blurred a little of the detail. She had a hint of the feminine, just at the edges. No curves, though. She was polygonal—skinny but rectangular. Simple math, simple design. Isolating one feature at a time, she was on the right path. Taken as a whole, she put me in mind of Marilyn Manson.

Turning my eyes downward, regarding myself from on high, I lost even that. Still the familiar too-gentle swell of my breasts, the scar beneath my solar plexus from a childhood bike accident, the belly beginning to pooch out thanks to too few home-cooked meals. And that's far enough down.

Across the room, centered in the oval frame of the mirror, Lita slumped her shoulders. A blade's width of polished glass divided our worlds. More than once

I had thought about taking that blade, turning it so the keen edge would cut me out. Not to hurt myself—those thoughts began to slow and sink the night of Shasta's party—but to rescue something from inside.

Or at least to switch places with the girl in the mirror who, upon closer examination, seriously needed to pluck her eyebrows.

I pulled myself together from a few disparate parts—laundry, vanity, fantasy—and headed to work. I had made it a habit to get to work twenty minutes or so before clock-in time so I could check my e-mail and browse the net. I could have probably afforded a cable modem for my place, but couldn't get over the feeling that doing so would be like inviting the world into my private spaces. It's a bad analogy, and a worse argument, I know. Here's a better one, at least argument-wise: the Internet at work was fast, free, and—given that the IT department, a guy named Charles, was a big privacy nut—largely unmonitored.

The first thing I did when I got to my cubicle was log in to my bank account. Not a whole lot there. If I squinted, the decimal point blurred away and I felt a little better. Either way, I had enough for this month's meds. Buried deep in my bookmarks was the site for my supplier, under the heading "Flowers." I clicked through.

This site has been blocked by eSafe under the heading: phishing/scam.

Oh, Charlie—Not a convenient time to change the network. I tried refreshing the page, but the same warning popped up. For a moment, I considered strolling over to Charlie's office to explain to him that, no, this particular Canadian Internet pharmaceutical distributor was perfectly legitimate, proof positive if you care to hear the details. I figured that wouldn't get me anywhere, except maybe on his bad side. He was a fan of privacy, like I said, but that also meant he was a fan of you keeping your privacy to yourself.

Instead, I logged into a forum I had joined after Victor's accident. It was under the title "Flower Chat" in my bookmarks.

It wasn't a super active community, like some of the others I had lurked in, but I got the impression that the people behind the names cared about responding to each other more than the anonymity of the net made necessary. I hadn't contributed much beyond an introduction and a brief word of encouragement to a girl making her transition, but it was comforting to me to consume the shared experiences of distant people whose stories shared a few beats here and there with mine.

Fifteen minutes went by as I checked up on my favorite threads, finishing up with one called "Why do you feel beautiful today?" No new posts since the last time I had checked, but I re-read the most recent, which was from a boy in some big metro high school.

Because my drama teacher gave me unlimited access to the spirit gum and facial hair collection. It made me smile, and wish—not for the first time—that we humans could trade bits and pieces of ourselves.

Joy arrived in heavy boots and a bright yellow windbreaker. Her house was a ways out of town, getting into the mountains near the pass. Droplets of water clung to her hair.

"Snow already?" I asked, closing my browser window and reaching for my headphones.

"Oh, just a little dusting," she replied. "It's coming, though. I keep telling Billy he needs to get the genny fixed." Billy was her husband, a man whose faults I had learned well in bits and pieces.

"I'd be all right with some snow," I said. "I think I was eight the last time we got anything more than a couple inches at once."

"Young enough you didn't have to get to work in it." Joy grinned at me. "That was back in El Niño times? Or La Niña? It keeps changing."

I shrugged, smiling. "Beats me. I like your jacket."

"It's warm. Billy got it for me when we took that trip to Disney. He said it was either this or a hunting vest. Didn't want to lose me in the crowd."

A couple of the other transcriptionists filed in. Before diving into the day's work, I thought I'd ask: "Hey, did they do something to the Internet?"

"Is it down again?"

"No, I just got this weird message from something called eSafe."

"Oh, yeah. Charles mentioned that in the last manager's meeting. It's a company that keeps a blacklist for us. Out of Charlotte, I think. What were you trying to get to?"

"Nothing important." I felt a blush grow outward from my cheeks and kept my eyes glued to my monitor. After my face had cooled, Joy began shuffling papers on her desk. I knew she had filed away the moment, carefully labeled. It might never be recalled again, but I couldn't help the suspicion that if I ever did get her to pull out her mental file on me I'd find way more than I could remember.

I buried the thought under a stream of verbal short-hand from the emergency room docs. Bee stings, spider bites, an accident with a table saw. Pretty routine stuff, no admissions to the inpatient floor. A convict had come in for a tetanus shot. The doc on-duty for that one had a Garrison Keiller voice, reporting dutifully that the patient "denied any family history of mental illness" after describing a trunk wound that bore all the hallmarks of self-infliction.

Five seconds into what promised to be another brief report on one of our frequent flyers, the voice of one of the front desk girls cut through the intercom: "Code Yellow, ER. Code Yellow, ER. Code

Yellow, ER. Was that–" The signal cut off. Joy glanced up at me. *Code Yellow* meant a big trauma, mobilizing the safety team to the command center. By "safety team" I mean a reluctant volunteer from each department, and by "command center" I mean the administrator's office. I had attended one of the mandatory quarterly meetings of the safety team, before my transition. The agenda had focused on power cords and the dangers they posed as trip hazards.

"Probably a drill," said Joy as I pushed away from my desk.

It would have been the first, though I could swear that I had read something in the bylaws about requiring a drill every six months.

Hauling open the heavy stairwell door, though, and stepping out into the main hall it was clear that this wasn't a drill. Men and women stood in the hall, some on cell phones, some just leaning against the walls, most meeting my eyes briefly and then looking away. I guess my confusion showed on my face. The things you can miss when you spend your day in the basement.

On my way to the administration hall I passed the front desk. The girl who had called the code, blonde and fresh out of high school, was shuffling papers madly, the printer behind her clattering away at full speed. I wanted to ask her what had happened, but the line in front of her desk held what little of her attention was still available. Nobody looked particularly ill or wounded from what I could tell. Some of them looked bored. It probably wouldn't have been the best plan to ask one of them what happened, either. Especially with my employee badge so visible on my lapel.

I pushed on through an *Employees Only* door and into the administration wing which, given that we had a whopping two executive types, wasn't much of a wing. Maybe a buffalo wing.

The administrator was on his phone, listening and nodding. Two big plastic totes, labeled *Code Yellow*, sat on his desk, their lids off, their contents half gone already. One held a dozen brand-new walkie-talkies. The other was full of bright orange safety vests. Two other safety team members were hunched over the conference table; I recognized the nurse manager, who had her cell phone up to her ear and a few pages of spreadsheets splayed out in front of her.

"Can you be here in fifteen minutes? OK, thank you!" She sounded bright, positive, and fake.

Across from her was a guy I had seen in the cafeteria a couple of times. A respiratory therapist, if I remembered right. He was ripping walkie-talkies out of their clamshell packaging and popping batteries into them.

"Reporting for duty," I muttered, not intending for anyone to hear me.

The administrator cupped his hand over the phone receiver and said: "Yes?"

"I'm on the safety team. What happened?"

He nodded, spoke a couple of affirmations into the phone, then beckoned me over to his desk. Again he covered the receiver. "Put on one of these." He handed me a vest. "Just direct people away from the ER." The phone slid back up to his mouth and he carried on his conversation, rattling off some numbers. I gave him a thumbs up.

Turning, I noticed that the RT was watching me. He beckoned me over.

"School bus accident," he whispered.

"Yes, you get paid overtime," muttered the nurse manager into her phone.

"Is it bad?" The RT shrugged. He was about my age, or at least right around my fashion era. Two pale lines ran back from the corners of his eyes to his sideburns, shadows of sunglasses worn during a tan.

"Collided with a logging truck. They airlifted the driver out to Sacred Heart already. Doesn't look bad for any of the kids, last I heard. Just kinda crazy." He handed me a fresh walkie-talkie. "Channel three. Make sure you don't flip over to four; that's reserved for the EMTs."

"Aye aye," I said. He smiled and, from that angle, his tan lines looked like broad extensions of his laugh lines.

The safety vest fit me exactly like a potato sack. I looked at the tag on the collar. XXL. The seams stuck out a good six inches from my shoulders. I felt as if I were wearing a power suit. Evidently, it made a similar impression on the bystanders, because as I made my way to the door to the ER wing two different families stopped me to ask about the accident. Can we see our daughter? Is our son all right?

To the first, I tried to claim ignorance and begged their patience, angling myself awkwardly through the crowd. To the second, I just said: "It'll be OK."

The big double-doors to the ER had been closed and locked. Only an employee with a badge could get through them, so I wasn't sure what good I would be doing, but nevertheless I positioned myself right in their path. Hands in pockets, at first, then crossed in front of me, then crossed behind. None of the options seemed natural.

A young mother, carrying a baby in a sling, approached me bashfully.

"I'm sorry, sir, but is there any update?"

"Not yet. I'm afraid I don't know much more than you." The words were about as out of place as my posture. An apologetic smile fit much better, and after seeing it the young mother nodded and padded back toward the cafeteria, bouncing her baby gently. Someday, Jilly would be riding the bus to school. That put me in a much more sympathetic mood, less self-consciousness, and I think I came off better, calmer, more appropriate to the next couple of concerned parents who came to me hoping for an update.

After fifteen minutes or so, with nothing much passing through my post but a portable X-ray machine and a couple of radiology techs, I slumped against the wall and let the weight off my heels. The young mother caught my eye as she peeked out of the cafeteria hall, but I gave her a slight shake of my head. I felt like a robot, but not too bad about it. Simple programming. If anyone requires feedback, request patience; else slouch. A strange comfort settled on me, a Nuremberg refuge. I have orders. I follow them. I stretched the feeling like a pair of nylons, pulling it outward. If I felt comforted by that, how much more comforted then when the instructions become so much more complex. Stacks upon stacks of directions, written there by responsibility, society, hormones. A fractal density of programming which must contain at least a few mistakes. Either that or I was and will be perfect.

The analogy snapped, or rather I snapped out of it. The RT from before gave me a nod from across the crowded waiting room and headed my way. When he got within earshot he held up his walkie-talkie and tapped it.

"I think yours is off."

I had jammed the thing in my pocket and forgotten about it. Sure enough, the power light was off. I blushed, and honest to god worried how bad it clashed against the orange vest. "Sorry. Did you try to call?"

"Chris did, yeah." The administrator.

"First name basis," I noted, though I'm not sure why. It earned a weak smile.

"Yeah. You can probably turn your vest in, now. They're going to start letting the families in a few at a time."

"Oh, good." I pulled my arms in through the short sleeves and started to wriggle out of the thing. It obscured my vision as I lifted it over my head. When I could see again, the RT was grinning at me. "What?"

"Ever see *Flashdance*?"

I laughed, tried really damn hard to make it a giggle. "I'm not sure how to take that."

A middle-aged man, heavy set and bald, brushed past us and grabbed the handles to the ER door. He was so purposeful, I almost didn't make note of it. The doors, still locked, didn't budge.

"Oh you have to fuckin' be kidding me," the guy grumbled.

"Excuse me, sir," I said.

He turned and sized me up. Sweat stained his arm-pits. He looked like a man who worked hard for his living. "Yeah, come on. Open up."

"They'll be calling you back real soon. Don't worry–"

"No, no. Open the doors." He gave the doors a hard yank. The rattle of the frame, pulling against the sturdy electromagnet that held it tight, perked up the attention of a few others in the waiting room.

"We don't have the key," said the RT.

"Bullshit."

"Sir, they're working as fast as they can," I said, kind of irritated at the guy's stubbornness more than anything else. "When they're ready– "

"I'm having chest pain, you fucking idiot!"

Magic words for anyone who works in healthcare. I glanced at the RT, but not long enough for him to give me any sort of feedback. "I'm sorry, sir." I swiped my badge in front of the lock plate. "Sorry." It beeped and with a heavy *chunk* the magnet disengaged.

"Fag," muttered the man, pulling way harder than he needed to on the handle. The door swung closed behind him. The magnet caught.

"Probably talking to me," the RT said quietly.

I balled up the vest in my hands. "We should go with him."

A beep, and then the door opened again behind me, pushed from the other side. One of the nursing assistants slipped out into the hall, holding a clipboard and propping open the door with her foot. "Collins?" she called, cleared her throat, called louder.

Through the gap in the doorway, I could see the chest pain man talking to another assistant.

A man and woman, I guess the Collinses, came up. "She's fine," the assistant told them, tapping on her clipboard. "Bed seven, if you want to follow me."

"I'll take that, if you want," said the RT, gesturing at the vest. I handed it over, robotically, still capable of following some instructions at least. He turned back and slipped through the crowd, which had begun to buzz and stir from the activity around the doors. I stared at my shoes. They were good shoes, more expensive really than I should have sprung for. They weren't showy, but they made my feet look narrower than they really were. The soles clicked down the tile hall and into the cafeteria.

A little covered porch extended off one end. It was empty except for a couple of women absorbed in their cell phone conversations, so I got a cup of coffee and went out to sit on one of the smooth metal benches. The air smelled like fuel. The two women, both angled so they faced the wall, each shared slightly different versions of the day's events with whomever was on the other end of their lines. It was maybe sixty-five out. A dry fall breeze moved through my hair, cooling my skin, reminding me how full of blushing blood it had recently been. A sip of coffee brought me back to equilibrium.

The door to the cafeteria opened and the RT slouched toward me, hands in his pockets. He held himself with a lazy confidence which I could only ever approximate through laziness.

"Are you OK?" he asked.

I nodded. "Sorry about that."

He shrugged. "Not your fault. Mind if I sit?"

I scooted over to make room on the bench.

He folded his hands in his lap and hunched forward. "Do you remember me?"

"Yeah. You're that guy on the safety team, right?"

He laughed. "No, I mean from school."

"You grew up here in town?"

"We moved here when I was a freshman. I was a year behind you." We both had to cock our heads to meet each others' eyes. "I'm Germaine," he said.

A memory stirred of a skinny kid with bad acne and hand-me-down clothes. "We had Bennett for history?"

"Yeah, we did." He grinned. It was the sort of grin I could admire, deep and toothy.

"They called you 'Germ.'"

"Still do."

"Sorry."

"I don't mind." He narrowed his eyes, as if in thought. "You apologize a lot."

I nodded. No point in arguing or apologizing for it. "Yeah. I don't let go of mistakes too well. I still can't believe I got a C on Bennett's midterm. Stupid me, couldn't remember if Grant was with the Union or the Rebels. Still can't."

"Same boat, here. I pretty much wiped the slate clean as soon as I saw my report card that semester. As far as I know, Attila the Great was the third Emperor of United England."

We both laughed. I clammed up quicker, self-conscious when I realized we had the same tone and timbre. I took a sip of coffee, scalding the roof of my mouth.

"I heard about your brother," said Germ. "I'm sorry."

"Did you know him too?"

"I hung out with the skaters and stoners, so, uh, yeah." For a moment, the blithe confidence in his voice wavered. "How is he?"

"Recovering. Seems awfully slow. The specialists don't seem too bothered, though. He spends a lot of time sedated."

"That sucks. It's going to be hard to shake that."

"Yeah. When he's conscious, they give him one of those morphine buttons."

"Do they know what happened?"

I shook my head, took another sip of coffee, kind of wished I had a beer. "The FBI came by to talk to us after reviewing his story. I guess they're classifying it as a hate crime, technically. Or investigating it that way, at least."

"Not as a gang thing?"

"I don't really know the difference. Probably just some different paperwork they have to file."

"There's some compensation from the state if it turns out to be a hate crime. All that morphine can't come cheap."

"No, you're right. That'd be nice. Mom and Dad would probably appreciate it. I know I would. Listen to me. It'd be 'nice' if my brother's torture were considered a hate crime."

Germ smiled. "I know what you meant."

"Yeah. I just—" I tried to make the silence look intentional by swallowing another hot mouthful of coffee. "It blew away my savings. Mom and Dad can't be much better off. So much for my trip to Thailand."

I don't know if it was for his benefit or mine, but Germ seized on the new thread. "Thailand, huh? I've never been."

"Me, neither."

"What's in Thailand?"

"Good surgeons." I'm not even sure if my abruptness was designed to lead him further on or shut down his questions. It didn't really accomplish either.

"Sounds about twice as expensive as sightseeing."

"Yeah."

He drummed his palms on his knees. "Probably ought to check on how things are going."

"Should I go report in?"

"Nah. It's pretty much under control. See you later." Before standing, he tapped my knee with his palm, the cymbal crash at the end of his little drum solo. He went back inside and for a moment I felt completely lost at sea. I had no idea how the conversation had gone. I had no clue on what terms we were parting. More than anything, it scared me. I felt a nervous spasm in my gut that threatened to bring up the coffee. I felt for a moment like a bewildered audience of my own life and I wanted to leave the theater.

The rest of my coffee went down the drain. Victor's place made a much better cup. Back in the office, everyone wanted to know what happened. I shared my version, omitting the bald man and my mistakes, wiping out my involvement as much as possible.

6

One Saturday in late October, I got a surprise call.

"Lita? It's Jeanine. Want to go to the salon with me?"

I stammered out a "Sure," and she finalized the plans. I hadn't seen her for more than a month. Her treatments kept her in this weird state of always either being in Spokane or getting ready to go.

We met up outside Gracie's place at a quarter-to-eleven. Jeanine had a vivid pink scarf wrapped around her head. She gave me a hug and held the door open for me. It was quiet inside, which I always appreciated, but kind of felt bad about. Quiet meant slow meant it probably wouldn't be long before the shutters closed. Gracie brightened up when she saw customers, dialed it up even further when she saw it was us.

"Hi, ladies! What are we doing today?"

"How butch can you make me?" With a flourish, Jeanine unwrapped her scarf revealing a patchy mess of her old dirty blonde hair. Gracie's mouth made a little O of exaggerated horror. "No, it's fine," said Jeanine. "When I decided I was going to get it cut, I let Jilly play around with the safety scissors."

Gracie and I exchanged similar expressions and then we all three shared a good laugh. I pictured the scene, Jilly probably saying "Cut, cut, cut," as she followed her own instruction.

"Have a seat," said Gracie. She led Jeanine to one of the barber chairs and swung a black drapery around her shoulders. I plopped down in the chair next to them. Gracie scraped her fingernails across Jeanine's scalp, like a sculptor getting the feel for the grain of a log.

"So, how are you feeling?" I asked. My feet swung beneath me, the chair a bit further off the ground than I was expecting. It made me feel like a kid.

"Morose and horny," said Jeanine. "The treatments are killing me."

Another shared laugh and my cheeks began to threaten a cramp. "Testosterone's a bitch," I said.

"Tell me about it! I had them write down everything that they're pumping into me. Half of them come with a risk of decreased libido, according to the

Internet. The other half say they might increase sex drive in women. I know which half is winning. Of course, that also comes with loss of bone density, hair, sense of smell, and there's the whole cancer thing. Funny, though. I've got a colony of rogue cells setting themselves up as a dynasty, but I just want to fuck."

Gracie blushed. "Language, grandma," I said, clucking at Jeanine.

"I'm serious! But at the same time, I can't help but think that it's not going to make anything better, that it won't satisfy me. Still. Just my luck, though, I wouldn't have the strength to do much but lie there."

"Nothing wrong with that." I fidgeted with my legs, feeling all the more like a child for having such an adult conversation. "Shasta told me you had a boyfriend."

"I'm afraid he's out of the picture. Can you believe he was married? Scumbag was cozying up to me at the treatment center, stringing me along. The whole time he had a wife back home, terrified that she was going to lose him to the cancer. Jerk."

"Brace yourself," said Gracie. She clicked on the electric clippers and began to buzz them through what was left of Jeanine's hair. It took her only a couple of minutes, then the scissors came out for shaping and trimming around the ears.

"Can I ask you a personal question?" Jeanine asked, catching my eye in the mirror.

"I'd feel kinda left out if you didn't."

"How did you pick 'Lita'? I mean, it's pretty—"

"I love it," Gracie chimed in.

"—but there has to be a story behind it. I mean, not everyone gets to pick their own name. The rest of us kind of settle into them."

"It's a short story," I said.

"I don't want to pry. Well, I do, but—"

"No, I don't mind." I smiled, found the lever to lower my chair, and slipped it down until my shoes hit the tile. "It's short for 'Carlita.' Which is the Spanish feminine form of 'Carl.' Which means, uh, 'masculine.'"

Gracie's scissors clicked like the second hand on a clock. Then Jeanine burst out laughing. "Oh, I'm sorry," she said, bringing her hands out from under the drape and wiping her eyes. I couldn't help myself from smiling and then Gracie, taking her cue from me I guess, joined in.

"But mostly I just like the way it sounds." That brought an aftershock of giggles.

"It suits you," said Jeanine punctuated with a stifled snort. "I'm sorry. I feel like I'm on laughing gas. I don't know what it is."

"No, I totally agree."

"Does my daughter know?"

"She hasn't asked. It's not really her kind of humor, you know? Besides, it's more of a buried story, now. It's my name, and you'd have to really wear it out to expose the joke. I guess the good thing is if I ever get sick of it, there's nothing stopping me from changing it again."

"Good point! I'm tempted to try that myself. I could be a Danni. Or a Lindsey, maybe? I've always liked the name Silvia."

"You know those are pornstar names, right?"

"Seems appropriate," said Gracie, immediately widening her eyes in shock. "I'm sorry, I didn't mean that." We drowned her out with another round of laughs, which only took her a bare moment to join. Behind the humor, I felt a weird shiver, a feeling I had always put together with the phrase *walking over my grave*. But it was kind of the reverse, a sensation of something walking over my childhood, passing ghostly through the very memories that life had stacked end on end to reach its current height, and finding them somehow altered or rebuilt. Jeanine had been my girlfriend's mother, a specter haunting all our young games with the call to come back inside, to eat our vegetables before we could watch a movie. We had ducked and dodged her, planned our days like spies around her patterns so we could have the most fun and, as we got older, so we could get alone in a bedroom.

Then she was the grandmother of our daughter. She had held Jilly close in the hours following her birth, dueling politely with my mom for the honor. Lively, distant, elevated; a respectable professional who had spent lots of her time on the road since Shasta turned fourteen. Less time traveling after Jilly was born. More again, now.

"Did you ever play the piano?" she asked me. I had been fidgeting with my fingers in my lap but hadn't noticed. "You have piano fingers."

"Nope, sorry. I can't even lip sync." I grinned. "They're just going to waste."

"All done!" said Gracie, brushing off the nape of Jeanine's neck. The mirror gave us back nothing that might have shown up in glossy print, unless maybe you cropped out the corner with Jeanine and me. Still, Jeanine seemed happy with the result. Instead of a straight buzz, Gracie had given her something much more pixie-like. The hairs were short, but flowed together to create a sense of motion, a shallow wave. It wouldn't last; patches would show up as they treatments continued, but right then it looked pretty rad.

"Your turn." Gracie ushered me into her chair and shook out a fresh drape. I know I have a tendency to weigh down the lightest moments with unnecessary observations and flat fugue miseries, so it's important to note that the next few minutes were blissful, empty. The sun shone at too low of an angle to burn. Geese honked, high in their Vs heading south. Rare traffic brushed a layer of white noise, overtop of which Gracie's scissors clicked. I wasn't in much need of a trim, but I never would turn down a little styling.

"Your hair is so healthy!" Gracie knotted her fingers through it and gave the back a little shake. "You hardly need product at all."

"Thanks! I made it myself."

"We could try bangs. Do you want to?"

"'I dunno. What do you guys think?"

Gracie pursed her lips and folded a length of hair over my forehead. Jeanine tilted her head first to one side, then the other.

"No," they both said at the same time.

I laughed. "The jury has spoken." Gracie went back to snipping off my split ends.

"Hey. How's Vic doing?"

"You're the only one he let call him that." I smiled at her reflection. "He's OK. Mom and Dad went up there yesterday. I was thinking I'd day-trip it tomorrow. Do you want to come along?"

"I don't know." She let the words hang and fall. "I don't think he wants to see me. He hasn't returned any of my calls or texts."

"He still can't really use his hands," I said gently.

"Oh." She studiously avoided making eye contact and her cheeks flushed. "I forgot."

"It's OK. He forgets sometimes, too." It was a weak attempt to lighten the mood, and gravity pulled it down quick. "Can I ask what happened between you two? I was all hoping I'd get to have a sister-in-law." Strike two on the humor. Gracie's face fell a little further, then seemed to reach a steel core. She set her mouth in a thin line.

"The night before, I caught him dealing to one of the Indian kids down the street."

"Not cool," said Jeanine.

"Please don't tell him I told you. I mean, I know it's illegal, but it's just– it's just awful." Jeanine and I both nodded. I was agreeing not to tell; I'm not sure exactly what she meant. "That was right before we were supposed to go to dinner at your parents' house. We fought, hard. You know one of those where if you've kept anything at all bottled up, it comes out? He shut down after a while, just stopped fighting back. Finally he told me it was time to get ready to go. I went to the bathroom and heard the front door slam. He just took off. The next thing I heard– " She put down her scissors.

Neither Jeanine nor I said anything for what I guess was too long for Gracie's comfort. "There. You're all done."

"It looks beautiful," I said.

"Please please don't tell him I told you."

"Of course not." I undid the snap on the drape while Gracie stood there with her arms folded and her eyes cast down. Climbing to my feet, I opened my arms to her for a hug and she fell into them. She was shorter than Shasta, the top of her head nesting right in the crook of my neck. "It wasn't your fault, if that's what's in your head," I murmured.

"No, that's not it. I'm just– my heart is just sick, not knowing how he is, or how he's feeling." She sniffed and drew away. "You know?"

"Yeah, I think I do. You want definite answers."

She chuckled softly. "I guess. I mean, I'd rather know that he doesn't want me than leave all the hundreds of maybes out there to choose from. I go through them all, one after another."

"What if he doesn't know?" asked Jeanine, with a delicacy to her voice I had never heard before. "If both your hearts are flailing, what are the chances they'll catch and hold?"

Gracie nodded. "It's why I haven't called him. He doesn't need that."

"Do you want me to ask him?"

She shook her head. "No. Really, no." She paused, and seemed to be reading the inside of her mind. "But tell him I hope he's feeling better. "

"I can do that. I'll do it when Mom's not around, so she doesn't start badgering him. She's pretty fond of you, I know that. Got a rock solid heart, too."

Gracie laughed and wiped the corners of her eyes. "I'm sorry, girls." The door to her shop opened. "Hi!" she called to her next customer. "Just have a seat and I'll be with you in a minute."

We followed Gracie around to the counter, where she rang us up and, already beginning to chat with the next lady, failed to notice when we both tipped way too much.

Outside, the cold was beginning to gather into gusts and I swear I could smell snow. Jeanine shivered and rewrapped her head in a scarf.

"Bad time for a summer cut," I said, but whatever chemical or social drug had been swarming our spirits before had dissipated. I earned the ghost of a smile. "How do you feel now?"

"Like a million bucks, give or take. You?"

"Would you believe morose and horny?" I asked.

"Sadly, yes. We're in a strange place, you and I, kiddo." She opened up for a hug, her arms still plenty fierce despite whatever the cause and cure were doing to her.

"Take care of yourself."

"Yeah, that's my best option. Give Jilly a hug for me and tell Shasta I said hi."

"Will do."

It was snowing by the time I made it home.

7

What's it called when you daydream at night? I lay there awake in the dark, unable to track the progress of time from the faint static light of the streetlamp. It bisected my closet door just left of the middle, unbalancing the room. I imagined I could hear the hiss of falling snow. For a while, I lay on one side until I decided I had never been more uncomfortable. I switched to the other side. Before long, I realized that, no, now I was the most uncomfortable I had ever been.

There is no way to impose any sort of rigor on the images that parade in a half-awake mind, not without coming fully to. To maintain any hope of falling back asleep, you have to let your mind play out, never mind how painfully it limps through quiet internal armageddon stories.

Acid snow fell on the street, trees, and lawn. It melted, and the land beneath was barren, its features changed beyond recognition. I saw Jilly walk toward me from the distance and never grow any larger. Dust and hair. Sandstone and wire. Shasta played the piano for me. She never learned how. A sculptor placed us all in a kiln and let the temperature rise and linger until all our imperfections hardened into stone.

Impassable time trickled by me, a dam made entirely of water. Shasta unbuttoned her top and handed it to me. I expected kindness; I saw lust. She knelt and held me in her mouth and I pulled myself completely out of dreaming. The thing I had come to view as my tragically inverted vagina was hard and I needed to release the pressure. I reached down and found come slicking my skin and underwear, my cock already softening. Every patch of skin on my body— whether it seemed foreign, mine, or newly mine— burst alight with irritated nerves. As though I was fevered, my skin felt as if the slightest touch would bruise it.

Wiping my hand on the sheets, I turned to look outside. The snow—no trace of acid—had piled up and was still coming down. The small of my back ached, right in the place that I had come to associate with the onset of illness. I slipped out of the panties and T-shirt I had worn to bed and went to draw a bath.

The water couldn't get hot enough for me. I was hoping for the kind of heat that leeches into your bones, melting your muscles along the way. I got something closer to lukewarm, but still at least above ninety-eight-point-six. With the tap still running, I slipped into the tub. Slowly, the water level rose to cover my hipbones, then rushed over the great plain of my tummy. The tub wasn't long enough for me to stretch out, so I had both legs crooked to one side, knees up. In that position, I could tuck my thing between my thighs and relax. Just relax.

The lights snapped off so suddenly I thought that a bulb had blown. I reached for the tap and twisted it off. The flow of water slowed, then stopped; the last drips plinked into the water. I considered getting out, but what the hell. Nothing wrong with taking a bath in the dark. I collapsed back, sending a wave sloshing end to end. I glanced over toward my bedroom, and squinted when I found I couldn't find the red glow of my bedside clock. The flow of air from the vents had stopped, too. No hum of refrigerator.

"Awesome."

I climbed to my feet, wrapped a towel around myself more for warmth than modesty, and went to check the breakers. They were all good. I clicked the main off and on a couple of times, as if it would help. Nothing.

I peered out the window. The weight of snow had bowed the trees across the street, and the lines between telephone poles had lost all their tension, looping dangerously close to the ground. None of the apartments nearby showed any signs of life. The only light I could see came from the streetlamps; their amber glow suffused the air, filled as it was with prisms and mirrors.

The fire station's siren woke slowly, sounding forever to me as if it had to be cranked by hand like a World War II air raid device. I went to my bedroom and put on a pair of flannel pajamas, then returned to the living room and set myself up by the window. I caught, then released, a strong desire for a cup of coffee. All my appliances were electric.

Staring out at the storm, trying to imagine the weight of all that water pressing in from all sides, I could almost feel the wind pass straight through the glass in front of me. As if the cold were so tiny, the force so direct, that it could make its way between the molecules. I shivered and hugged myself.

Fully awake, beyond committing to sleep, my mind brought up an image of fire and held it, taunting, while my body cooled.

I went back to bed, back to my comforter, but I didn't sleep any. Every so often, I looked over at my clock, hoping to see it start flashing midnight numbers but its face remained blank.

8

The next morning, I got a call on my cell phone from Joy. "Don't worry about coming in. All non-essential staff get a snow day." Good thing, too. We had gotten almost twenty inches of snow over the night. Worse still, a glaze of ice had covered everything. I had gone out a bit before the call, weighing my options for getting to work, and had found my car frozen under a layer an inch thick. I could have walked, I guess. In the light of day—which, honestly, was not that much brighter than the light of night had been—it was easier to see the damage, and to feel a part of it. Power lines, phone lines, tree branches, everything sank under the weight.

The city's snow plows were running as best they could, but it was clear that it would be more than a little while before they got to my street. I bundled myself up good, filled a couple of gallon jugs with water in case the pressure died, and once again set myself up in front of the window.

I tried the number for Victor's room, but no one answered. It was a long shot, anyway. He couldn't hold the phone himself, and so only picked up when a nurse happened to be there to lend a literal hand. I wondered if Spokane had been hit as badly. My phone could browse the web, but it was slow and everything showed up strangely formatted and small. Still, with nothing better to occupy my time, I dug deep and found the patience. A couple of inches had fallen at the Spokane airport. Nothing about an ice storm. Just finding that out chewed through twenty minutes and about fifteen percent of my battery life. I had maybe a third of a charge left.

My phone rang, startling me. It was my parents' number.

"Hello?"

"Hi. It's Dad. Just checking up."

"Hi, Dad. I'm good. You sound tired."

"Long night. Storm caught a lot of people on the road."

"Anything serious?"

"Nope." In the background on his side, I heard Mom's tin pots and pans clanking. For a time long enough for me to start counting, neither of us said anything. Then: "Your mother's making campcakes if you can get down here."

"Oh, man." Victor's and my childhood word for the secret, sweet pancakes that Mom would make on our occasional weekend trips to the mountains, the coast, or wherever Dad wanted to pitch the tent. "I'll plow the road myself if I have to."

"I fired up the Coleman. I'll tell her to double the batch."

"Dad," I said. I heard a note of enthusiasm in his voice, the same as he used to get when Victor or I would agree to go tramping through the forest with him, or follow him into the freezing Pacific, or anything other than stay comfortable at the campsite. I had to dampen it. "What about Mom?"

"She's doing fine."

I don't think it was the answer to the question I had asked, but I decided not to push it. "All right. I'll have to hoof it. No way I'm getting my car unstuck in this mess. I'll dig out my snowsuit and see you in a while."

"See you soon."

I found a pair of heavy snow boots lurking in the back of my closet, along with big shapeless mittens and a ski mask. I decided against the ski mask. Whatever pants I chose were going to end up soaked through, so I layered a couple of pairs of sweats. I stuffed my pajamas into a coat pocket, so I'd have something to change into, and checked myself in the mirror. Bad idea. Not the worst, but still bad. I felt and looked like a kid on his way to go sledding, not at all like a girl on her way to visit her parents.

Before I stepped out the door, I checked the time on my phone. Just barely six. It felt so much later. I wasn't surprised, then, not to encounter anyone else on the road as I kicked and stomped my way down the side streets to my parents' house. No one out shoveling the walk; no one sweeping drifts off their roof. Blinds were drawn, with no movement behind them.

The snow absorbed all sound below a certain threshold, somewhat louder than a whisper. It was as if all distance had disappeared. Noises couldn't reach; clouds bunched over my sight lines. Isolation and stillness, almost dreamlike. I felt I was floating. I wouldn't even have been able to tell my feet were hitting the ground if they weren't hurting, half-numb. At least my fingers, all bunched together in the lobster claw mittens, stayed nice and warm.

Dad had shoveled a path from the road up their front walk. He hadn't scraped all the way down to the concrete, but at least it made the walking easier. I felt salt crystals crack under my feet. Mom answered the door.

"Come in, come in," she said, irritated maybe that she even had to say it. "Take off your boots. The deicer ruins the floor."

I stripped off my coat, kicked off the boots, yanked off the mittens. "I need to use the bathroom."

Mom waved me off and headed toward the kitchen. Dad was sitting on the couch, feet up on the coffee table, seeming to watch a dead TV. "Hi, Dad." He waved with his bad hand, three-fingers. I changed quickly into my pajamas and came back out to sit next to him.

"Sure smells great, Mom," I called. She didn't answer. "Anything good on?" I asked Dad.

He shook his head. "The PUD got iced up bad. I guess we've still got lines coming in from the dam, but most of the city runs off stuff sent up from California, and the substations all down the valley are toast."

"That bad?"

"It'll be a couple days at least to get the whole city back up."

"Anyone hurt?"

He nodded, but didn't elaborate beyond that.

"Breakfast time," called Mom.

Dad and I sat on one side of the dining room table, Mom opposite. She placed a steaming plate of campcakes between us, a kettle of coffee and a pitcher of orange juice flanking it. "Thanks, Mom." We dug in. The free association in my brain took me to Christmas morning, or an amalgam of all Christmas mornings. She had never made us campcakes for Christmas. I guess my poor memory was confused by new experience. The cakes were delicious, hearty and thick. The coffee was perfectly strong. The orange juice cool and refreshing.

The three of us were silent.

An engine grated outside, and we heard the telltale whine of tires finding no traction. Dad leaned toward the window and peeked through the blinds. Finishing his mouthful, he said: "The Johnsons across the street." He put down his fork and pushed back from the table.

"Where are you going?" asked Mom.

"We've got a bag of cat litter, if they need it," he replied. Mom and I both returned to our food while Dad put on his boots and coat. He slammed the door behind him, but not out of anger; he just had never seemed able to shut a door quietly.

"Good breakfast, Mom," I said into the silence afterward.

She nodded. I cursed myself a little. Mom had never been great at accepting compliments. Bad way to strike up a conversation. A gulf had opened between us, that was obvious, but I hadn't thought it had divided me so far from remembering how even to act around her—how to coax out a smile, how to really show appreciation, how to say all those things that as a child I knew by intuition.

"Mom?" She looked up from an intense study of her fingernails. "Are you mad at me?" Forget the intuition, the hedging around. This was a woman who wore out a wooden spoon on our young behinds. Nothing that I might consider part of my adult character could possibly matter to her; I was a child. I would never be older than her, never even be as old.

"I'm not mad."

"You're something."

"I'm letting you have your space. Jesus had his wilderness. You have yours."

I nodded. Eventually, most everything came back to God for her. I kind of envied her mind with its closed loop, its predictable paths. Each strand of thought perfectly traceable, each fiber of energy with one discrete origin and one end. "I'm sorry," I said. My mind was much less organized, more like another set of arteries and vessels with the core of my mind pulsing raw nervous indecision to capillaries, tendrils, stumps of ideas, phantom limbs.

"How is Jilly? We need to see her again."

"She's fine, Mom. She's got so many words, now, I can't even believe it."

Mom nodded to herself, drew in a deep breath. "Has her mama got anyone lined up? Girl needs a daddy."

"I don't know, Mom." We could have ended the conversation there, and lapsed into silence until Dad came back from his mission of mercy. But, no, my heart and brain pumped hot blood and anger. "It's not going to be me."

"You love her, don't you?" She shot me an accusatory glance.

"Yes! I love both of them. But it's not... Never mind." I felt suddenly so thirsty I drained an entire glass of orange juice in one gulp.

"Then I don't understand. Are you gay?"

"Yeah, Mom. I am. I'm a lesbian." For being a word that stood in for me, for my identity, I sure made it sound a bit rougher than I should have.

Mom's eyes went hooded and darkened a shade. "I'm trying to understand," she said.

"Are you, really? I feel like you're missing a big part of this picture. You're trying to wedge me into some category you're comfortable with." There was a spark of pride with that last. She didn't respond immediately. The silence ballooned, expanding to fill the whole room, until I punctured it with a small: "I'm sorry."

"I'm trying to understand. You don't give me time to understand. Child, you want all the answers right away, with no room to wiggle. You had years to learn, but you kept it to yourself."

My stomach clenched. I had no argument against her. Still, though I could have replied with another apology, I said: "You had the same amount of time."

This time the silence lengthened and had no interruption. Mom pushed back from the table and began to clear away the dishes. The front door creaked open, pans clanked in the sink, but it was all perfectly silent. As Dad kicked off his boots and stamped up the hall, Mom gave her last word: "Woman was created as a companion to man."

I couldn't take it. Across the street, the Johnsons' truck finally caught traction on the pavement. They made it down the block and around the corner without getting stuck again. Good for them. I finished my coffee and joined Dad on the couch in the living room. My phone said it was almost seven. There was snow in Dad's hair and he smelled kind of like wet dog.

"We've got a call with Victor in a couple of hours," he said.

"I'll stick around."

After a few minutes Dad, never able to keep still for long, climbed to his feet and went to build a fire. As the kindling caught, I remembered that I hadn't taken my pills yet, my routine in shambles thanks to the long night. Then I remembered that I only had one day's worth left, that the refills were supposed to arrive in the mail that day.

"The mail's not running today, is it?"

"I doubt it," said Dad.

We watched the fire together. Gray light filtered through the curtains. The pop and hiss of boiling sap came to my ears like a bedtime story. I didn't know what would happen next. I fell asleep.

The next thing I knew, my phone was buzzing and ringing in my pocket. I panicked, believing in my drowsy brain that if I missed the call I would never get another. How many times had it rung already?

"Hello," I said, indistinctly from a gluey tongue.

"Jilly's gone. Did you take her?" It was Shasta's voice, but the tone was wholly unfamiliar. Panic and accusation mixed together. The solution seemed unstable.

"No. No— she's gone?"

"I can't find her anywhere." The accusation boiled away, leaving the remainder purified. "Mom's checking with neighbors. God." Her voice poured into me, and I felt it right away coating my stomach, my muscles seizing up.

"Dad," I said. He had left me alone while I slept. "Dad!" I heard a low mutter from the direction of his bedroom, the walls blocking the words. "We're on our way. Keep looking. I'll get Dad to call rescue. Hold on."

"OK." As Shasta ended the call, I noticed I had only a sliver of battery life left. I was on my feet and heading to my parents' bedroom when Dad met me coming the other way.

"What's wrong?"

"Jilly's gone missing."

He froze, met my eyes full on. "During the night?"

"I don't know. We have to—" It probably wouldn't have mattered what I said we had to do. Dad nodded, brushed past me, found his work phone on the counter and dialed. He had a quick conversation with whoever was on the other end, mentioned getting one of the city plows.

"Get on your stuff," he said, hanging up. "They'll come get us in the rig."

The fire siren growled, hummed, then sang out clear through the cold air.

After climbing back in to our winter gear, Dad and I waited at the end of their driveway, like children waiting for the school bus. Before long, a yellow dump truck came around the corner. The blade affixed to its grille tossed powdery snow in a wide fan. Dad motioned me back so I wouldn't get buried as the plow slowed and stopped in front of us.

I pulled myself up to the cab and slid in. The driver—an old man who looked as if maybe he was retired but for plowing—gave me a nod, then leaned around me to talk to Dad.

"Ought to take us about ten minutes, the way the roads are. I was partway up the grade when they called, so we'll go that way and finish 'er off."

"Mornin' Frank. Sounds good." Dad slammed the door behind him. The cab smelled like cigarette smoke, and had no seatbelt in the middle for me. I don't know if it was to show solidarity or just because his mind was elsewhere but Dad didn't fasten his belt either. He got on his phone and made a couple more calls, giving out the address and checking on his team's whereabouts.

That only took him until we made it to the grade, where Frank had left off his plowing before.

"Hit that switch, will you darlin'?" said Frank, nodding toward the dash. I flipped the switch on, triggering a small amber light and a long hiss from the back as the spreaders spun up, casting dark sand behind us.

"She might just be hiding in the house," I said to Dad.

"Let's hope so."

As we turned onto Shasta's street, we passed Jeanine, shapeless in layers of coats, stepping out the front door of one of her neighbors. She looked up and waved, but I'm not sure she knew it was us. She was just about the only sign of life we had seen on the whole drive.

Frank slowed to a halt in front of the house. "I'm headed back out to the highway. Call home base if you need me again."

"Head back along the cutoff, in case we need to drive out that way?" Dad gestured up the unplowed stretch of road.

"Sure thing," said Frank. "Good luck." He touched his hat brim and we both slid out to the ground. Jeanine had caught up to us.

"What happened?" I asked. Dad, spying flashing lights headed our way, stepped out into the street after Frank's rig had cleared away.

Jeanine's words came at a pace slow and separated, each word freezing and alone. "Shasta and I, we both slept in this morning. When I got up around eight to make the coffee, I noticed the front door was open. Jilly wasn't in her bed, and we couldn't find her anywhere."

A county pickup with the Fire and Rescue emblem on the doors pulled up and some of Dad's old colleagues piled out of the extended cab. Dad stepped in and took Jeanine's elbow gently in his good hand. "Where have you looked so far?"

"Just the neighbors. Shasta's out in the orchard. I couldn't find any tracks."

"If the snow was falling—" I began. Dad shifted his hand from Jeanine's elbow to mine and squeezed.

"OK." Dad looked at his crew. "Three-year-old girl, blonde hair. Name is Jilly. Jeanine, you get a bath tub and anything warm ready. Lots of blankets. If we find her on foot, we bring her to the closest house. It'll probably be here. Lou and Reg, take the truck, scout from the road. If you spot her, it's straight to the hospital." A red SUV pulled up beside the pickup. Germ slipped out of it, wearing a big blue jacket with the stenciled word *Volunteer*. He gave me a small wave and then turned his attention toward Dad. "The rest of us, we'll walk a grid out from the house. Quarter mile to start with. Let's go."

"I'll help Shasta with the orchard," I said as the men began to split up. Dad nodded and started to forge his way across a bare, white alfalfa field toward a low hill a quarter-mile off.

"Safety committee wasn't enough for you?" Germ said, giving me a slight smile and a bump on the shoulder.

I smiled back, just as slightly. "You, neither?"

He headed off, slogging into the shin-high snow of an empty pasture.

I made my way toward the orchard, my layers of pants already soaking against my skin. The bark of the trees looked black against the canvas of the ground, like sumi ink. I peered down each row, feeling like a child in a supermarket trying to find which aisle her parents had vanished down. Shasta's footprints led all over; even if I fancied myself a tracker, I'd have been no good tracing her path. Finally I saw her, a black down ski coat above skinny jeans. I hurried up to her, calling out. She spotted me, waited, and turned for a hug. Before I caught her, I saw that tears had frozen her lashes into spikes.

"It's OK," I said. She sobbed into my chest. "Everyone's here. We'll find her."

"I stopped calling out." She sniffed; her nose sounded clear, dry, but I figured that was because the snot had turned cold and solid. "Every time I opened my mouth, I thought what if it was right at the same time as she said something."

"Don't do that."

"I know. I shouldn't."

"What happened?"

"I don't know. She got the door unlocked."

"How did she get the chain?" I swear that at the moment I said it I was honestly baffled how our little daughter had managed to climb the doorframe, undo the safety chain, and slip out the door. The confusion didn't come across in my words or my tone. Shasta backed out of my arms.

"I didn't put the chain on last night."

"Why not?" No longer bemused, now I began to feel an anger stoked in my gut. A small action, an expenditure of so little time could have corrected this course.

"I forgot, OK?"

"Of all the nights– "

"You know what? I've tried to be supportive and quiet, but I'm way past letting you treat me like you know better how to be a mom." Her eyes narrowed, my anger banked. She seemed to search for more words and found them. "You're not a mom, and you'll never know what I'm going through right now, or any goddamn day of the week. You can't know. And you can't fucking judge me for something you'll never know. I don't care what you want to be. It doesn't mean anything to me."

Silence. She choked back an angry sob, turning her ear to the wind, maybe searching for the echo of an imagined call.

"She's my daughter too, Shasta. Maybe if you tried—"

"Fuck you, Simon. Just shut up."

And she didn't even notice what she had said.

We parted after a few quiet seconds. She turned first and headed down another orchard row. I made for the end of the property, for a blank acre of field beyond.

Stepping quietly, hoping to hear a whimper or a soft "Hep," I trudged in a straight line. Thinking how pitfalls could be hidden in the wide unbroken snow. A ditch, or a little girl in her pajamas, hidden by the sharp sameness of everything until your perspective was just right or you put your foot right in it.

My toes began to go numb. I realized that snow had been falling into my boots and stopped for a moment to pull the cuffs of my pants down around them. Shasta called out for Jilly. She sounded much closer than I expected, but no, she was gone and going in the other direction. Voices rise and fly unobstructed in the cold. The cold makes everything clear.

I put my head down and continued on through the field. With no features to the ground beneath I couldn't track my progress or even my motion. My mind disconnected and gave up trying. The only way to tell how far I'd come was to look back. Dad had said to cover a quarter mile out from the house. I couldn't judge the distance. I just kept going.

"Jilly!" My voice may have traveled far, but the snow swallowed up all the echoes. I was there the day she was born, the two of us full of promise and promises. Shasta gracious enough to let us all come visiting, careful to explain to newborn Jilly: "Here's your Auntie Maria." Mom didn't say a thing, didn't care what she was called. She melted on the spot as Jilly slept in her arms.

"I don't want to make things harder on her growing up," Shasta had said. And I, so keenly aware of just how much shit I had piled on her shoulders, would have agreed to practically anything. It was almost a relief that her request was so large, so deeply sunk into our lives. I would not be Jilly's father or her mother. That was enough to repay what I felt I owed Shasta, and I agreed with gratitude on my face.

So I was Uncle Simon for a little while, Mom was Auntie Maria, then I was Auntie Lita. Somewhere in between, Shasta gave me her graduation gown, we walked together, and even held hands.

I reached the edge of the field, marked by a two-strand barbed-wire fence buried up to the second strand. I paused and wrapped a mittened hand around the steel. It hadn't been enough for Shasta, me giving Jilly up. Was that because I didn't show, or fully realize, how much it had cost me? Or was that cost just not enough to balance? Like with most everything in my brain, I figured it was kind of both. Two sides of a coin, ground up to a powder. It's a shame that the almost palpable knots of confusion in the mind can't be teased out by a good surgeon. I would have made an appointment right then. The Thailand trip would have to wait.

For the first time in more than a year, I thought about hurting myself. The thought was unbidden, but I really should have seen it coming, standing as I was all gloomy with my hand right next to the frozen starburst tangles of the barbed wire. Puncturing a hole, drawing an incision in the skin, it was as close as I had ever come to removing the confusion. One hole, one deep slice, and the threads of failure and regret find their way gently out, driven by the heart. It was always a release; the pain was a secondary distraction.

"He's got her!" A voice I didn't recognize echoed off in the distance. "He's got her!"

I froze.

My thoughts went white. I saw flashes of movement between the crooked apple tree fingers and I turned and ran as best I could, finding my own footprints and sending sharp crystals of snow into the air.

As I reached the orchard, I heard an engine turn over. I caught a glimpse of Germ's SUV, backing into the narrow lane the plow had left and then accelerating out of view. Trees whipped past me on either side. It was taking forever to retrace my steps; I hadn't thought I had gone so far. I burst out of the trees and saw a bunch of the rescue guys milling around, Dad with them, his radio up by his jaw. He spotted me and met me partway in a big hug.

"It's OK. She's OK."

"What—" I gasped with a deep, dry cough.

"She was hiding out in a barn. Cattle kept her warm."

"Are they taking her to the hospital?"

"She was conscious, circulation was good. Shasta and her mom went along with Germ. Lou and Reg are on their way back with the truck."

"She's OK?"

Dad smiled. He needed a shave. I probably did, too. "Yeah. Smart girl."

The truck pulled up and everyone piled in; two guys hopped into the bed to make room for Dad and me in the cab. "We're headed to the station. Bound to be more calls. Drop you off at home first? Fire's still going, I bet."

I shook my head. "Can you take me to my apartment?"

"Heat's still out."

"I'll be fine. I just want to get some things together before I head to the hospital."

"She'll be in and out of the ER in no time." When I didn't reply, Dad slipped his bad hand over my shoulder and gave me a squeeze.

He was right about more calls coming in. Halfway down the hill they got another, a car spun out on the highway. The city plows had got most of the main arteries with at least one pass, so another crew was on their way. Still, his face was glued to the radio when the truck came to a stuttering halt in front of my building. He waved me off. One of the guys in the truck bed swung around to take my spot.

My apartment was as dark and cold as it had been all night. I ran the water in the kitchen to bring a bit of feeling back to the tips of my fingers. I struggled out of my boots, stripped off my damp clothes. I took my blankets to the couch, like getting ready for movie night. Wanting to check the time, I found that my phone was completely out of juice.

It was gray outside, a darker gray inside. The only color came from behind my eyelids. I let them close, forced them to stay there until a fitful sleep turned even their canvas monochrome.

9

I woke up to pain in my bladder and a fear of open spaces trailing me out from dreamland. After a trip to the bathroom, I looked outside. Heavy clouds had gathered while I slept. Even if I had had a working clock, my internal one would have been way off thanks to the dusky quality of the light. I wanted badly to call Shasta and Jilly, and I suppose I'm grateful that the circumstances made it impossible.

With nothing to keep me occupied at home, my mind cast around for distractions. I remembered that Mom and Dad were supposed to have a call with Victor. Dad was probably still out working, but I could at least check in with Mom. My stomach grumbled its agreement, the campcakes long gone. It's stupid to say it, but I just about blew a gasket right there at my tummy having a mind of its own. If each part of me would just settle down, obedient, and listen to instruction, keep its voice in check, not speak until spoken to, I could have a life of peace and progress.

Seems reasonable to suspect that missing my pills had something to do with my mood; then again, it had only been a single dose so far, so maybe it was all in my head. Either way, steps had to be taken to address each unruly piece of me. I nibbled on a cereal bar to soothe my stomach, not sure if Mom would really be in the altruistic cooking frame of mind, given how our last conversation had gone. I got dressed, tucked myself in properly, and shaved with cold water and soap. I did a little something with my hair, put on some foundation, and popped a pair of green glass studs into my ears. Little things, each, but afterward I felt like me again without even looking in the mirror.

I pulled on a pair of thick wool socks, some clean jeans, and a sweatshirt. I hadn't done anything with my boots, so they were still damp like trenchfoot and kind of smelly. I figured I would be able to keep out of the deep drifts well enough, so laced up a pair of tennis shoes. Then coat, hat, scarf, and I was good to go.

The air outside was cold but thick, making me think that a good yell might not travel as far as it might have that morning. There was a moisture that reminded me of a long night in bed beside someone, breathing, sweating under the sheets. The snow was a thick down comforter on the Earth. I took a deep breath.

Even being as careful as I could to watch where I stepped, my shoes were soaked through by the time I made it to Mom and Dad's. Mom answered the door and stepped aside silently, letting me pass. The fire snapped from the living room, chewing up the oxygen in the air. Everything felt close and warm, like being smothered in a favorite blanket.

"How's Victor?"

"He's OK," she said over her shoulder, on her way to the kitchen. She had dug out a blue plastic drying rack. I had interrupted her in the middle of wiping off the dust. "They want to send him home."

"Back here?"

"Well, he can't take care of himself yet." She pulled out a huge cooking pot and began to dump in jugfuls of water from repurposed gallon milk containers. "Not going to happen today, but the doctor thinks some time this week."

"You need help?"

Mom capped up the jugs and held the pot out to me. "Sure. Go put this over the fire." I tried not to show my forearms shaking from the effort as I carried the brim-full pot over to the fireplace. Mom had positioned a cast-iron stand over the flames; the pot nestled snugly into it.

"No, I meant with Victor."

With a flick of her wrist, Mom turned up the gas on three of the burners on the stove, laying out a griddle over two of them and another, smaller pot on the third. I finally thought to check their grandfather clock and noticed it was nearly dinner time; I had slept the day away. Mom puttered around with flour and oil, opening up the dark fridge for just a split second, long enough for her fingers to dart in and snag an egg.

"Mom?"

"What?"

"Are you guys gonna need help with Victor?"

"We'll manage."

I could only remember a handful of times that Mom had lied to us, as children. They were usually so outlandish that she couldn't have hoped to pass them off as the truth. No candy on long car rides because sugar makes you have to pee. No R-rated movies because they make it so only adults can hear the soundtrack, so why bother. No swearing because it turns your tongue black and everyone will see what a potty mouth you are.

This one, so small, almost slipped by me. It made me wonder if all this time she had been playing a game with us, feeding us huge unforgettable lies so that we'd be distracted from others. My eyes began to sting with the threat of tears.

But if my eyes held the threat, hers held the promise. She turned away from me and bent over the sink. "The investigators found out that Victor used to run with those bad kids, fighting with the Indian boys. There's nothing from the state when it's not a hate crime. I told them he gave it up years ago."

"You lied to the FBI?"

"It's not a lie!" She spun to face me. Sadness and anger dovetailed with no visible seam. "It was a phase he went through, but he grew out of it."

"OK," I said, even raising my hands, palms out. Mom returned to mixing whatever was in her bowls. "He made a bad choice or two. We'll do what we can. Sure."

"I can help with Victor. I kind of know how to talk to people in a hospital."

"I said we'll manage." From the living room, the sound of boiling water blended with the crack of hungry flames. My eyes felt exactly as hot. Mom glanced up at me, back down again almost before I noticed. "You could do the dishes, if you've got room in your schedule."

I nodded, not fully trusting myself to speak even one syllable without cracking. I retrieved the pot from the fireplace, plugged the sink drain, and poured the scalding water four inches deep. Steam billowed up into my nostrils and eyes; I felt it clean my pores, ducts, and veins, rushing through me. My hands submerged, I worked with a scouring pad on the morning's campcake dishes.

Partway through the pile, Dad came home.

"It's coming down again," he said by way of greeting. "Could be worse tonight." I peered out the kitchen window. Sure enough, though dusk was gathering I could see bright white flakes slicing through the air.

"How bad was it?" I asked.

Dad gave Mom a half-hug and a one-way kiss. "Even working all night, power's gonna be out until late tomorrow at the earliest." He dug in the hall closet for the half-dozen mismatched kerosene lamps we had used during outages and storms ever since I could remember. "Hey," his muffled voice called, "something smells good." He set about refueling the lamps, trimming wicks, lighting them and positioning them around the kitchen and living room. The smell transported me instantly to childhood, to the night of a big storm when I was in fourth grade. I wondered if sometime in the future the oily scent would make me remember today, or if the link back to my grade school years remain a constant.

"The mayor set up a temporary shelter at the theater," said Dad, returning to the kitchen and dipping his hands in my wash water to clean off the oil. "They've got generators going and some heat, food, and water. I said I figured we'd be all right here, but I might go lend a hand setting up."

"After supper," said Mom.

"Course."

I finished with the morning's dishes right around when Mom finished dirtying up the evening's. She piled hers up and said: "I'll get these." My hands felt huge and fumbly after so long in the hot water. At the table, Dad grabbed one and Mom the other and she said grace.

We had mashed potatoes, dumplings, and chicken soup. Wiping my bowl with the last bite of dumpling, I said: "Wow. I've eaten better today than I have in a long time."

"You're too skinny," Mom replied, nodding.

"Thanks, Mom."

Dad wiped his mouth on his napkin and pushed back from the table. "OK. I'm heading to the theater. Coming with?" he asked me.

"Is there anything I can do?"

"Always something for a volunteer."

We bundled ourselves up, said goodbye to Mom, and stepped out the door. A warm wind caught me by surprise. It felt like a sick, hot breath. Snowflakes surged and dropped in its gusts.

Dad had driven one of the department's rigs home. I climbed into the passenger seat. "Shit," he said, settling into the driver's seat.

"What?"

He flicked on the windshield wipers; they jumped slightly but couldn't move beyond that, stuck in place. "It's gonna be freezing rain."

"Got a scraper?"

"Nah, don't bother." He turned on the engine and then the defroster full blast. "We'll just go careful." We made our way down the street at a crawl. Even going so slowly, the truck's back end fishtailed the first time we made a corner. "It's gonna be a busy night."

The theater was only five blocks from my parents' house, but it took us a full ten minutes by the dashboard clock to get there. We only saw one other car on the road, a little Camry heading straight down Main so fast I hoped the driver didn't want to make a turn any time soon. "Busy fuckin' night," said Dad.

We got out of the truck and I just about lost my footing on the first step. The tendons on the inside of my thighs sang out and I swore. Dad came around the cab. "You OK?" I started laughing a little, and he joined in.

"Yeah."

"Watch that first step."

The generators were in the alley behind the theater, clattering away, all pistons and fuel and metal fatigue. They chugged and hummed; the sound blended right into a few dozen conversations as we pushed into the theater. It was packed harder than opening night for a summer blockbuster. Dim overhead lamps and footlights giving a dreamy orange glow to everything. The rows of padded red seats were bolted in place, but the armrests raised up so that folks could stretch out in a sleeping bag or wrapped in blankets. The narrow stage, leftover from before the place showed moving pictures, held a row of tables with gas hot plates and stoves. A line of people with camp cookware snaked around, shuffling past the ladles and dishing themselves up. A pallet of bottled water sat off to one corner.

"Looks like they got things under control," I said.

Dad nodded, raised a hand to someone he knew off on the other side of the room. Children laughed and ran up and down the aisles, the whole night shaping up to be one glorious sleepover. I breathed in other people's breath and liked it.

"Hi mister Hernandez, Lita." Germ came up to us.

"Hey," I said. "What are you doing here?"

"Volunteering." He smiled at me.

"Did you hear anything more from Shasta?"

He shook his head. "Not after the hospital discharged the girl. That was a long time before the weather turned again, so they're probably back home nice and snug now. That was a smart girl," he said with unhidden admiration. "Crawled right under the hay. I woulda been dead scared of getting kicked by one of those cows."

"Yeah. She's a smart girl."

"I'm really glad she's OK."

We all shared the sentiment, but neither Dad or I had much to add. A small cough of static came to me in stereo, followed by a whine. It took me a second to realize that the sound was coming from Dad's radio, and a second more to figure out that Germ had one, too. A voice came through the speakers, fast and muddled; I couldn't make it out, but Dad picked up on it well enough to swear out loud again. Twenty-odd years, and I had never heard him use the F-word so much.

"That's way out there," said Germ, after the radio had quit.

Dad held up a finger, spoke a brief response back to the dispatcher, then returned the radio to its belt clip. "I've gotta go," he said to me. "Want me to take you back home?"

"No, I'm OK here for now. If you think Mom needs me—"

"Doubt it." Dad gave me a smile that meant more than I could figure at the moment, then headed back outside.

"You're not going with him?" I asked Germ, trying to sound as neutral as possible. I didn't want him to think I was eager for him to take off; I didn't want him to think I was desperate for him to stay. As if I had much ability to influence what other people thought.

Germ shook his head. "That was a two man response. Volunteers like me are only supposed to go to full calls. Otherwise we get in the way." He grinned.

"Gotcha." The truth was: I was more than a little glad he hadn't gone. I was fighting a resurgence of the feelings I had had that morning with my fingers on the barbed wire fence, though instead of making a hole in my skin to let the confusion drain I felt the impulse to turn it all into words, even if they didn't make sense, and cast it out of me by way of my tongue.

"Hey, are you feeling all right?" Germ asked.

I shook my head. "How could you tell?"

He smiled, held it until I looked up and took it in. "Just a feeling. I'm a champ at reading into things. Come on." It's not like there was a quiet corner for us to sit and talk, but sitting down next to him in the back row of creaky red seats I did feel that pleasant isolation, just like going to the movies. A shared isolation. He lowered an armrest so he'd have something to lean against and turned toward me. "So what's up?"

"It's been a bad day."

"No shit." I searched his face in the dim orange light for a hint of condemnation, but found none. "We'd make a good team," he said. "You're the understater, and I'm the overthinker."

"I kind of feel like the overthinker."

"Yeah? Want me to give you an example of me doing it? It's good and embarrassing."

"In that case, go right ahead."

"When I was a sophomore in high school, I almost came out to my parents."

"Wait– you're gay?"

"No, not at all. But I had a crush on you and that confused the hell out of me, I'll tell you what. Threw me for a loop for the whole damn year. I got real depressed, and finally decided I'd have to tell my folks that I must be gay, or at least that I might be bi." He paused. His eyes twinkled and I could hear a warble in his voice. "Then the rumors about you started flying. And when graduation came and you wore Shasta's robe, it started to make sense."

"Oh my god. I had no idea."

He shrugged. His smile reappeared, "Can you imagine me telling my folks: 'Hey. I think I'm gay,' and then a couple weeks later coming back and saying: 'Actually, he's a chick, so never mind.'"

Everything started twinkling again. "I'm really sorry."

"It's really not your fault."

"Germ." I opened and shut my mouth a couple of times. There was a great pressure of words trying to get out, but I guess the block wasn't there at my lips or teeth. "I'm not into guys."

He nodded, shrugged, nodded again. "I had a sneaking suspicion."

A middle-aged man edged into the row in front of us, gave us a polite nod. He wedged himself up against the wall and curled up, fully-clothed, under a rough green blanket. The distraction dissipated my conversation with Germ, who had turned in his seat to face the screen.

"It's OK," he said. "You don't have to worry about hurting my feelings. In case you were. All I'm feeling is a bit of admiration for you. I mean, even back then I thought you were something else. Courageous not to give a damn at the rumors. I remember thinking how much braver you were when the rumors turned out to be true."

"I don't know," I said. I felt my head filling with blood and tears and getting heavier. I slouched down into my seat and tried to speak so quietly. "I just don't. I haven't been able to do a thing right. And not like I've seen the options and picked the wrong one. That'd be OK and I could hate myself for that and learn, you know, for the next time something similar came up. But it's just so unfamiliar. I feel like all the territory is new and I wasn't— I'm— I wasn't born for this."

Germ nodded. What else could he do, really? I've got no analogy for how it felt to speak. It was the reverse of how it ought to have felt. No physical model made sense. Speaking, letting out the words, just crammed more pressure into me. I wanted to scream, instead, maybe give that a shot.

"I need to sleep," I said.

"I'll leave you alone," said Germ.

"No, I can't sleep here. I think I'm gonna go home."

"Oh, OK." He crooked a smile my direction. "Can't say I blame you." Our neighbor had begun to snore.

"Um. Do you have your car?" I asked.

"Yeah. You need a ride?"

"Please."

I had a few minutes to cool down, to try to find some better way of encoding my feeling than in ineffective words or Jilly-style hollers, while Germ went to let someone know where he was off to. Then a few more minutes as he and I scraped down his SUV's windows and door handles, then another ten while we inched down roads that had shelled over with solid ice. Not that any of the extra time did me any good.

"I'm sorry," was all I really had for him when he pulled to a halt in front of my building.

"Hey. Sit with me for a sec," he said. The heater was on full blast, and truth be told I was dreading the effort to warm the dark insides of the apartment. He kept his hands on the wheel, staring straight ahead. "Think maybe this is what it looks like when hell freezes over?"

"Maybe," I said.

"OK. I told you I read into things, so you just cut me off if I'm making shit up, but I don't think you should be alone tonight. You've been beaten to hell today, and there's not a bit of it that was under your control, and that kind of scares me. I know what happens when someone thinks there's nothing they've got power over. They dig until they find something." He searched my eyes, glowing faint blue in the dashboard lights, I think looking for some sign that he should shut up. He didn't find one. "I don't think you met my sister, Katie. She's six years older than me, already graduated when we moved into town.

"My folks were pretty religious. Mom was super strict with Katie when she was in high school. No dating, ridiculous curfew, no parties. Katie and the pastor's son got together. I don't think it's right for me to tell the whole story, but she did some stuff without my parents' knowing. Word got around and it kind of forced us out of the church, and led to Dad looking for work over here." His voice lost most of its tone as he went on further.

"Anyhow, if I thought my parents were strict before– well, hell. It was bad. Just think if I'd come up with the courage to come out of the closet, even if I did take it back later." He smiled ruefully. "Mom and Dad said: Our house, our rules. They may as well have put an ankle bracelet on Katie. She'd have these big outbursts some nights, just mood swings like you wouldn't believe."

"I might."

"But I guess that wasn't the worst of it. I mean, the outbursts you could kind of see coming. Really, what else are you going to do? I flew off the handle once or twice, too, when I thought they were being unfair. Trouble is, I thought that was the end of it with her. I thought that's how she fought back – asserted her control and her independence and whatever other psy-chology catchphrase I felt so damn smug for knowing back then.

"That wasn't it, though. That was all show, all big clouds of smoke. Mom and Dad always won the argu-ments, if getting the last word counts. And then she'd go sulk in her room and I'd give her some space and it wasn't for months of this going on that I found out she'd sneak into the bathroom and quietly get the last say, chucking up her dinner.

"I hate throwing up, you know? Hate it. Put it off as long as I can, whenever I get a stomach bug, even though I know you feel better afterward. But she got it down so smooth, so quiet, I wouldn't have ever known except one time I was standing right outside the door when she did it and made a big deal to her about not wanting to catch her germs."

"What did you do?"

He shrugged, flipped the wipers on. Even with the defroster on full blast, the blades had frozen at the base of their arcs. He clicked the switch off again. "Nothing. I didn't understand. Didn't help. She's probably grateful for it, but we don't talk much anymore."

"She's OK?"

"Yeah. She finally moved out while I was away at college. I don't hear from her a lot. But you know what I learned? All that pressure – whatever you're feeling – it's got to come out. It's going to come out. You're gonna find something you can control, something you can change, and you're going to change it."

I shook my head. "I can't think of anything." It was getting kind of stuffy in the cab. "I've got this picture of myself– I mean, I've got a lot of them, and some of them I'll never be, but– it's like I'm a ceramic girl. Molded, cast once in a whole lot of heat, and now not really able to bend or grow. I can paint on all the layers I want, but I still don't feel like anything but empty. Just insulated and – I don't know. I just don't. I'll break. I just want to wipe out all the things I know and let the important ones find their way back. Just blast away all the nooks and crannies that my shitty choices have left clogged up and be fresh, lifeless, and new."

"Don't say that."

Too hot. Way too hot. My tears stung, but were cold compared to the air. I gave a humorless laugh. "Which part?"

"Sorry. I guess say whatever you're feeling." I didn't have a response. "You know, I think I'm stuck," said Germ.

"You are?" It may have just been because of the high density of emotion in my skull but I'd never really felt so incredulous that it made me angry, until then. "You could get a job anywhere. Probably get a girl anywhere. And why are you back here, anyway, if you had such a bad time with your folks?"

He caught my eyes and gave a reluctant smile. "I mean— I think the car's stuck." He pressed gently on the gas. The tires spun up then slipped, overcoming the little friction, rocking the car with the slight back and forth of bleeding momentum.

Stupid snot dripped out my nose and I laughed. Gratefully, he joined me. He dug between the seats and came up with a travel box of tissues.

"Does your phone work?" I asked him, after getting myself cleaned up.

"Yeah, I think so." He pulled it out of his pocket, checked the battery level, and handed it over.

"Thanks." I dialed Jeanine's home number. Sick, for now, of thinking about myself. She answered. I said I was sorry, so sorry, and hoped Jilly was doing OK. I heard soft words in return. Jilly was fine. Shasta was fine. Jeanine was drinking wine, which I knew she shouldn't do with her pills. Speaking of—

"I'm not pushing this thing," I said to Germ, hanging up and handing back his phone. "But I bet the beer in my fridge is colder than ever, if you want to come up."

"Yeah."

We got drunk, and told each other drunk stories of our lives. One day tardy on my pills, but they were still in me; I could feel them in my blood, making me dizzy and sensitive and I drank up the sensations, uncaring. We sat on the couch, feet up off the cold floor. I brought blankets. The night ended; the storm went on.

Part Three: Stick Indians

10

It was more than a week before things got back to normal around town. Final tally: seventeen auto accidents, six thousand homes without power, countless abandoned vehicles, the city's entire salt reserves decimated, and three deaths. One was an older native guy who I only knew by his reputation in the ER, named Jimmy King. Jimmy never came in alone, always had a cop under his arm. I knew all the diagnoses from transcribing his encounters and could guess the charges. Drunk and disorderly.

He had been caught in the storm the first night, when the snow came down heaviest. Walking somewhere, aimless and far. I don't think he had a home, or not a permanent one anyway. A kid found his body in a stand of trees, fingers in a death grip around a can of Coors Lite.

The other two deaths were my manager Joy and her husband. She had managed to get him to hook up the generator, but he'd pulled it right up in to the covered porch to make it easier to refuel. Overnight, the thing pumped enough carbon monoxide into the bedroom that they both suffocated.

Frozen to death and smothered in warmth. And we who just hovered in the middle, teeth chattering now and then, buzzed, body-hot and finger-cold, we did just fine. The only problem I faced was that it was a full week before the mail started moving again and I finally got my pills. I was climbing up the walls, nervous, convinced that the truck carrying my package had overturned somewhere, spilling its contents into the snow never to be recovered. I'd have to order another month's worth, and even then it would still be days before they arrived. But no, that was all fantasy and everything was fine. The pills arrived and my body went back to what passed for stable. I went ahead and ordered another month's worth anyway as insurance.

Germ was there for me whenever he had time, between his volunteer duties and his shifts at the hospital. He had gone back to work almost immediately, but I – and the rest of the non-essential staff – were out for almost a full week. A day after the power came back, Germ passed along that the management had requested we only come in if we had safe transportation. Then he offered to drive me in the next morning. I had woken up the previous couple of days with every intention of getting myself ready and then walking in to work, if I had to, just so I'd have something to do. But each morning I looked out the window and saw the gray sky, the filthy roads, and the sidewalks of mush, sand, and salt. That was all it took to tumble me back into bed.

"I work seven to seven tomorrow," said Germ "So I'll be here at six-thirty."

"Ugh," I said.

"It's either that, or we play hooky and go to the arcade. You're getting out of this house before it smothers you." I was pretty sure he had heard about Joy and her husband. Didn't want to confirm.

"The arcade shut down a few years ago."

"No way. See you tomorrow."

With the power back, my pills in hand, and a week's worth of time gone under the bridge I thought about calling Shasta. Lots of thinking, very little doing. I held onto my phone, kept waking it up and putting it back to sleep. Poor thing. Finally, I used it to call Victor. I was a little surprised when he answered.

"Hey."

"Hey," I said. "Didn't expect you to pick up. How ya feeling?"

"Like baked shit. I can use my hands, at least. They get the power back on over there?"

"Yeah. Mom and Dad call you?"

"Yeah. They had to convince the doc not to discharge me, since I didn't have anywhere to go."

"You guys didn't get the storm as bad."

"Nope." He heaved a great, big sigh. It sounded contented, like the kind of sigh you might let go after the first morning sip of coffee. "So what's going on with you?"

"Going stir crazy. Power's on, but most of the stores are closed."

"That sucks. TV day, huh?"

"I don't have cable, and nothing's coming over the air right now."

"I get sixty channels plus HBO and Showtime."

"Jealous."

"I guess that's why they charge the big bucks."

The humor was a little dinghy on a deep ocean of concern, its hull looking more and more like swiss cheese. I kept baling. "Not Skinemax?"

"Nah. You know my dick got burned off, right?"

"What?"

"Just fucking with you. Still there. They had to graft some dead guy's skin onto it, though. Frankenpeen."

"Oh, shut up I don't need to hear about your wiener."

He slipped another sigh and I could hear the creak of him adjusting himself in bed. "It's like heaven," he said after a time, kind of free-floating, anchorless.

"So." I hung onto the word, kind of hoping he'd pick it up and go on with some new conversation, because I didn't really have anything else that felt free enough to come. He didn't. "Mom and Dad coming to pick you up soon?"

"I guess."

Another silence stretched, and Victor's breathing became loud and even. "Vic?" No answer. I figured he had fallen asleep with the phone. "Love you, brother." I hung up. I killed the rest of the day by taking a long bath, watching a couple of DVDs, and arguing with myself about what sounded best for dinner.

The next morning, Germ showed up right when he'd threatened.

"You look nice," he said.

"Thanks." I felt refreshed, renewed, thanks in part I think to being able to return to a routine.

"Doing OK today?"

"Can't complain."

"I betcha could." He grinned, made a careful U-turn on my narrow street and headed for the hospital. The lanes were bare, but all the snow had been piled on either side, in some places looking ten feet high. The early hour and the walls of ice combined to form a feeling of wilderness isolation. I shivered. Germ's radio whined and a dispatcher's voice crackled through. He reached an automatic hand down to lower the volume.

"Are you always on?"

"Kind of. Supposed to be always available, anyway."

"Even when you're working?"

"Not usually, but I keep an ear out."

"What else do you volunteer for, anyway?"

He puffed out his cheeks and blew out a long breath. "I read to kids at the grade school; I'm part of the men's chorus; I do odd jobs at the church; and I sell Mary Kay."

"Joking?"

"A little."

"I'm jealous of your energy."

"Here's kind of how I see it: I'd like my life to be like that line from Neil Young. Better to burn out than to fade away."

"Kurt Cobain put that in his suicide note."

"Yeah, but he got it wrong. It's not about cutting anything short; it's about finding your boundaries. I want to do all this stuff so that when I finally hit my limit and my energy burns out, I can recognize that I've made it to the line. If I just sit around doing what I know I can handle, then I'll never actually know what I might have been capable of. I mean, sure, it's a life of no boundaries, which I'm sure feels pretty free, but it's stationary."

"Again: jealous."

"Yeah?" He turned to look at me, back at the road, back at me. "That's something." Back at the road. "Jealous just means you don't feel like you can do the same thing. It's not much of a motivator. No offense."

I shrugged. "None taken. Not like I have a rebuttal for you."

"I don't mean to make you feel bad."

"Think I would have survived high school if I was that sensitive?"

"Probably not." We pulled into the hospital parking lot and Germ took the first spot available, furthest from the door.

"But I should probably clarify," I said. "I'm jealous that you can get your life's philosophy across in the time it takes to drive to work."

He shrugged and half-smiled.

"No offense," I said.

"Yeah." He reached for his door handle. "I've gotta get clocked in."

Nice going, Lita. Open mouth, insert foot. "Germ. Please. I'm sorry. I don't mean that I think you're stupid or simple. It's— you know, like looking at a picture from your old photo books, and you think: Why can't life be like that again. Gleefully ignorant. You're not. I mean—"

He moved his hand from the door, across his lap, to rest on my knee. "It's OK. Just forget it. In a good way. I'm not mad." What followed was my silence to fill, but I refrained. We held that pose for a moment, then broke away, stepping out of the cab carefully onto the iced-up blacktop.

"Thanks for the ride," I said.

"Don't mention it."

"Too late."

He laughed. Our breaths froze quickly before our faces, condensing, falling without crossing the gap between us. "One more thing?" said Germ. "Let me know if I cross the line." I nodded for him to continue. "OK. Entropy increases; things don't get more simple."

"I don't know if that applies to humans, but if you say so. Haven't crossed the line yet."

"Wait for it." We stood right in front of the main hospital doors, which slid open for us, motion-activated. Germ stepped out of the range of the electronic eye and I followed. The door slid closed again.

"Things seem simple in those old pictures because, as children, we're stuck inside ourselves. Things are easy because we just don't care about the brains and hearts outside our own. We don't even know."

"I know," I said. A grain of irritation worked its way around my mind. "And simple doesn't mean good," I continued. "In my worst, knotted-up moments there are threads of good and bad and indifferent all woven together. Back then, as a kid, if there was something bad it was pure bad with no tint of salvation. The trouble is that sometimes I think I would prefer that, passing from thundercloud to silver lining without even caring how or even if they're connected."

Germ nodded, seeming to take my words to heart. I felt a bit guilty for not doing the same. "Yeah," he said. "I think I get it."

"Anyway. Still didn't cross the line."

"Bound to, sooner or later." He smiled and we walked into the hospital together, waved each other off at the basement stairs, and went our separate ways.

My office was dark save for the light from a handful of screensavers. I left it that way, finding my way to my cubicle on soft feet. From what I could make out, no one had touched Joy's desk. Something smelled floral, but only just— more like grocery store air freshener sprayed overmuch to mask a stench.

I logged into my PC and checked my queues for work. The ER had been plenty busy, even with the rest of the town shut down. I had way more work than I could possibly accomplish in a single day. Some days, that would have motivated me. Today I minimized that window and pulled up the net, clicking over to Flower Chat to read some posts until one of the other transcriptionists pushed open the door and flipped on the lights. I got my headphones in and hopped back to my queue before she made it to my cube.

"Oh!" she cried. "Sorry, Lita! Didn't see you there."

"It's OK." I smiled. Damned if I could remember her name. "I haven't been here long."

"Did you hear about Joy?"

"Yeah. Did she have any other family around?"

"I don't think so." We shared a slow nod, all eyes down. I imagined that her heart was beating the same slow pat as mine, sad, unobstructed.

"Couldn't stand being home any more, either?" I asked. Kelsey. Her name was Kelsey. She had transferred in from the purchasing department because she didn't like her manager there.

"I'm out of sick time," she said. "Not much of a choice."

"Well, good luck with your backlog. This is gonna take forever." I turned back to my screen and replaced my headphones.

Before long, a couple others joined Kelsey and me in the trenches. As eight o'clock rolled by we weren't much more than a skeleton crew. I typed up notes on hypothermia cases, first-degree burns, hatchet wounds. Jilly's case came up and flew away under my quick typing fingers, blessedly uncomplicated. Getting on toward eleven, a nurse—a friend of one of the other transcriptionists—came in and asked who was going to the memorial.

"For Joy?" I asked.

"That one's next week, I think," said the nurse. "This one is for Jimmy." I hadn't heard about it, but as it turned out Jimmy had made a lot of friends at the hospital on his many visits. Front desk girls, nurses, even a couple of the doctors had grown fond of the poor guy. A service of sorts was going to happen at lunch over at the community center a couple blocks down.

"I'll go," I said.

"They'll have Indian tacos," said the nurse, tempting those who hadn't gotten out of their seats.

◆   ◆   ◆

It was the nurse, her transcriptionist friend, Kelsey, and me at first, but on the sidewalk we ran into others, people I had passed in hallways and nodded and smiled at and had probably looked like an ass in front of in my big orange vest. Together, we took on the look of an honest-to-goodness procession, but it was far from a somber one. The conversations jumping from voice to voice like lightning, shapeless but directed, were the same that you'd likely hear in the cafeteria. Dull and lively. I followed a step or two behind my group. The snow and ice on the sidewalk had been stamped down pretty well, which was good for me since I hadn't worn my walking shoes.

The community center was packed. A set of three folding tables, draped in plastic picnic tablecloths, sat right by the entrance. Two cooks per table hovered over a little camp stove each. The sizzle and smell of fry bread welcomed us all to the quick-moving line. The last table held a vat of chili and a row of condiments to dress up our tacos. I couldn't remember the last time I had had fry bread. My eyes may have been a bit larger than my stomach, but it wasn't a condition I held alone given a brief survey of the co-workers and the other attendees.

After we got our food, we found seats in the grange hall. Nothing about the space or the audience made me feel as if I was at a funeral. I held onto a small, sad note of regret for Jimmy's lost life, but I admit that I felt a little guilty for it. Nobody else around me seemed to have it on their minds.

I ate slowly, my plate balanced on my knees, but even though I took my time and really had piled my plate higher than necessary I still finished well before anyone got up to speak. The first was a guy with silver-brown hair pulled into a long braid. The hall didn't have a stage, so I didn't get a really good look at him. He paced a bit while he talked, carrying a cordless microphone and occasionally remembering to speak into it.

"When we was kids, my cousin used to tell me all the time the stick Indians was coming to get him. Nights I slept with my auntie and uncle, he made me sleep under the window so they'd get me first. One night I asked him: 'Jimmy,' I said. 'Why you so scared of the stick Indians?'

"'They told me they were gonna kill me,' he says. Simple as that. Sure I didn't think he knew what he was talking about. Mama told me always the stick Indians didn't know words, didn't need 'em. But Jimmy, he was scared of 'em. Scared all his life." A gentle nod waves here and there in the audience, a minnow's ripple on a still pond. The speaker had to clear his throat a couple times, smoothing over some upcoming cracks.

"We all know Jimmy didn't take a lot of steps to help himself. But he never, never did stop walking. And he'd go ten miles in the snow for a cousin or a friend." The same minnow-ripple, this time spreading from a different point. "I asked him one time: 'Jimmy, why you still scared of them stick Indians? You ain't still believe in Santa Claus.'

"And he told me back: 'Because they hate us folk like me.'

"'What you mean?' I says. 'Like us?'

"And he says back: 'The first men. There were two of them and one stick Indian, and they kept a truce. But when the two men got lonely, they made a child, and one chose to be the mother and one chose to be the father. And so they had children. The stick Indian had no choice, all alone, and had to be both. It didn't want to be outnumbered, so it had to try and keep up. And so they hate us, all down through history, for being so many, and for being fathers and mothers.'

"And I said: 'But Jimmy, the stick Indians could just be mothers and fathers now, if there's enough of them. And he said right back in that kind of far away echo voice of his: 'It don't work like that.'"

I found myself nodding, adding my little part to the wave across the audience. Most everyone was smiling. I felt maybe I had missed some sort of in-joke. The speaker smiled. "It don't work like that, Jimmy. God bless."

Someone started a half-hearted applause, and after a couple lurches it caught on. I joined in. The speaker nodded his thanks and held out the microphone for anyone else. I sat through the next eulogy politely, though its tone was lighter and made reference to much about Jimmy's life unfamiliar to me. During the subsequent applause I rose and excused myself past my co-workers.

The walk back to the office was quick, quiet, and empty. I was alone on the sidewalk, and barely even passed by vehicles on the street.

Later that afternoon, Dad called up on my desk phone.

"Your brother's getting discharged tomorrow. Your mom doesn't want to drive on these roads, so was wondering if you'd go and get him. I've got to work tomorrow."

"She couldn't ask me herself?" There wasn't much purpose in me saying that, just about as little in calling it back, so I let it hang.

"That a no?"

"I can go, yeah."

"All right."

"What time?"

"They'll start the process whenever you show up."

"OK." The hiss of silence. "I better get back to work."

"All right. After work, you want to meet for a couple beers at the Lariat?"

He hadn't ever taken me out drinking before. On my twenty-first, he had had to work late, and I had hit the sack before midnight. "Um. Sure."

"Your mom didn't buy enough steaks for more than two of us is all. I'd invite you to dinner, otherwise."

"It's Thursday," I said, my sense of time catching up to me.

"Yep. See you around five?"

"OK. Bye, Dad."

I finished out the work day in a rhythmic trance of tapping keys. At quitting time, I was the only one left. Others had departed one by one as the afternoon wore on, citing the length of their drive, or needing to check on the kids. Kelsey was the last, apart from me; after she said goodnight and slipped out the door I got up, padded over to the light switch, and finished my work in the dark.

I caught Germ at his desk and told him I wouldn't need a ride home, that I was going to meet up with my dad. The Lariat was walking distance from the hospital, even under the circumstances. "OK. Call me if you need anything."

It took me about ten minutes on foot, stepping carefully on the unsteady geography that the ice had made of the sidewalks. The bar was full up, the tables about half so. I took a seat by the window. A girl in what I felt comfortable calling too much eyeliner tossed a coaster in front of me and asked if I wanted anything.

A craving hit and I committed. "I'll take a plate of seasoned fries and an ice water."

"Water, and sorry what?"

I leaned forward to repeat myself. "Fries." Once upon a time, it had irritated me how uneven my voice could sound when I tried to put some force behind it. I had been teased in middle school for singing in falsetto, but early after puberty started wreaking havoc I had learned that I could be my loudest in soprano. A blessing or an omen or something like that. The waitress nodded.

"Seasoned?"

"Please." I nodded, in case my voice still didn't carry.

While I waited for Dad, I fidgeted with my shoes. The tavern warmth had begun to melt whatever moisture I had picked up on my walk, and I was getting that itchy trenchfoot feeling on my skin. A tapping startled me; I turned to the window in time to catch Dad walking out of the frame, a careless finger lingering as he passed. A moment later, the door opened and he came over.

"Hi, sweetheart," he said. He smiled.

"Hi, Dad." My smile matched his, genuine, short-circuited around the conscious parts of the brain.

"How was your day?"

"Nothing too special. I went to the service for Jimmy King."

"Oh yeah?"

"It was different. More like a party, I guess. I don't know. I had to get back to work before it was over. Did you ever meet him?"

"He's that guy that sits in the park, yeah, on the bleachers? Watching the kids?"

"I don't know much about him, but he used to come by the hospital a lot."

"I think I ran into him a couple of times, if it's the guy I'm thinking of. He fell in the river, once. Said he tripped while walking over the bridge. Had to be a hell of a trip to clear the handrail. I fished him out a couple of miles downstream. Heavy son of a gun, all waterlogged. Had to do CPR."

"He had been drinking?"

Dad nodded. The waitress came by with my water and fries, took Dad's order for a Bud Lite. The fries were golden and crispy, a little mealy on the inside but hot enough that it didn't bother. I moved the plate so Dad could reach them too.

"Sober man wouldn't have pitched over the bridge in the first place." His beer arrived, uncapped and sweating bullets. He took a sip, then a longer one. The thread of conversation pulled away like an untended kite string in a summer breeze.

"Feels like wasted effort?" I asked, trying to reel it back.

He swallowed a mouthful, considering. "Nah. He survived the river, I mean. But I think maybe I'm getting a sense of how your mom feels about you two."

"What do you mean?" I took a big gulp of water, felt ice cubes touch off sensitive nerves in my teeth.

"I mean— I know I can't get involved in the lives of everyone I get called out for, but it's hard not to keep thinking on about them. That kid Scott pulled out of the sewer, you remember? What is he doing now with his life? Must be in high school or further on, now. And his mama, what's she doing? Everybody I've pulled out of a wreck or got clear of a fire. I don't feel like I'm responsible for them, but I feel something weird like needing to know they're OK." He took a long pull from his beer then set it aside. His hands folded as best they could. "Just so many people, like spiderwebs. And I made myself a part of their life, whether they wanted me or not. And sometimes I don't know what to do with that.

"But you kids, you and Victor— you're different to me. It's not that I care about you any less, but I look at you and I don't see a mess of webs. It's like every damn person in this world is a mess but you two."

I tried another fry. They had cooled. "We're pretty messed up." The grease had congealed on the shell and the insides tasted dry and bland.

"No doubt. But it doesn't screw with how I feel, is all I mean. Sorry this still doesn't sound so good. I've held onto it for too long. Kinda thought I'd be able to say it better by now."

"It's OK. I think I kind of understand."

"But your mama, she's a different story. You know she trusts the Lord for everything. She's that kind of faith that—don't ever tell her I said this—but you're not sure whether you oughtta admire or pity it. You know?"

I gave him a flat smile. "Childlike, but who says that's a good thing."

He nodded. "Yeah. That kind of thing. She does, by the way. And it's not up to me to argue. What I mean is that she's got faith and sees everybody in this weird clean way. Not sinless, but clear, and she knows just how she ought to act around them and how to think about them and what to pray for them. She knows that about everyone, never been a problem for her. Except for you two.

"This is her story, so I ain't gonna tell it right, I know. But she told me once how she felt looking at your brother in his crib, and it was sure a lot like how I just tried to tell you my feelings. She stumbled over the words, and she scowled, and she got so frustrated at herself, like she gets when she's hunting for a word she can't remember. Something's knotted up inside her when it comes to you and Victor." He finished his beer, wiped the moisture off the bottle. Then he sat there, looking at the water cooling on his palm.

"What do you see when you look at Mom?" I asked.

He took one of my fries, bit down, and made an unsatisfied face. "If I figure it out, I'm telling her first, kiddo."

"Fair enough."

"Best comfort I've got—and I don't know if it's for you or me, more—is that you've got to feel a lot of the same things as me, so we can share that without having to try and figure out how to say it as much. How I feel about you and your brother, I know you feel the same when you look at Jilly."

"That's different. I'm not really her mom. Not legally." I looked up and caught his eyes.

"You're not a great liar, girl." His eyes brightened and he smiled. "Not complaining. But you and your mama are the same like that. You both are piss poor at telling lies to other people, and dead on target telling 'em to yourselves."

My heart raced then slowed; my face flushed then drained dry. Dad reached out and took my hand. "I'm sorry," I said.

"You are your mother's daughter, no doubt about it." He started to chuckle; it was a few seconds before he clued me in. "I remember one time, god, you couldn't have been more than four or five. I came home from work, promised to play with you. It had been a rough day. I was tired and it was already getting dark out, but you wanted to play hide-and-seek so bad.

"I probably griped out loud about it, but we went out into the back yard and you made me cover up my eyes. I sat down on the back steps and counted and your mom brought me a beer. I probably counted pretty slow. Ninety-nine, a hundred. I stood up and heard you laughing, not even trying to hold it in. You jumped out from behind the woodpile. 'Here I am!' Then you ran back over and sat me back down and helped me cover up my eyes again. I counted, and this time as soon as I opened my eyes you screamed like a little monkey and shouted: 'Here I am!'

"Half-dozen times you did that before Mom called us in to dinner. Funniest thing I ever saw."

I leaned forward in my chair. My hair slipped out from behind my ears, half-covering my eyes. I was grateful for even that measure of privacy, from Dad and from the others in the bar. "I don't remember that." I didn't really trust myself to say much else.

"Yeah, you were pretty young."

"You should have come out and hid with me."

Dad's phone rang. It was Mom, wondering where he was and when he'd be getting home. He told her he was on his way. He let his hand rest on mine for a moment, then went up to pay. My guts tightened, seized up with envy toward people whose changes are inspired by the new, the unfamiliar, the necessary, instead of by a constant, helpless series of long-stale revelations. I have carried all of me inside of me and with me and not even known it.

I stood and caught Dad in a hug when he came back to the table for his coat.

"Drive safe, OK?"

I nodded. "I love you, Dad."

"Yeah. And I'm proud of you."

My head stayed down for most of the walk home. Dad offered to drop me off, but I thought the air would do me some good, or at least some not unwelcome ill.

◆　◆　◆

When I got back to my apartment, I ran a hot bath and undressed. Closing my eyes, I sank into the water. Gooseflesh raised all up and down me, and something else did too. Shasta's warm body had molded to mine, leaving no part of me cold or unloved. The water wasn't deep enough to cover my breasts; I raised my hands to cup them. For a moment, I suspended myself in a hybrid memory and fantasy.

Then my skin began to cool, hands and nipples aware that they were my own, that their heat was my own. The tub could hold a few more inches. I kicked on the hot water tap and let it flow.

The thing down there had picked up on my state of mind and had filled up to its full thickness. If I stood it up, its head broke the surface. I let it fall, let rest against my abdomen.

When I was a kid and bored in school, I used to play a game with myself. I would close my eyes and pretend that gravity was holding me up, that the world was inverted, that my desk was on the ceiling. It would take a few seconds to change my brain, but starving it of input always did the trick. The teacher would drone on, or a classmate would stumble over his tongue reading aloud from the textbook, and I would be fooling the pit of my stomach into seizing up with the fear of falling.

I tilted my head back, letting my ears fill with water. My heartbeat set the rhythm for my fingers; the only other sound in the world was the rush of water cascading from the faucet. For moments at a time, circling back on each other, my vagina was where it was supposed to be, in the configuration I expected. Then reality would return, and I would close my eyes tighter and think of Shasta's tongue against me. I moved my fingers in small circles across my clit, precariously balanced as it was on the end of my inverted tunnel.

My body shook, sending waves up to the height of my mouth. Now the tub was far too full. Then I reached for the faucet, let the ebb of sweet chemicals subside, leaned back, and died. Eros, then Thanatos, and bringing up the rear: whoever is the god or goddess of sick humor. I pictured myself from the outside, lying in the seed my body produced because it didn't know any better. Not my body's fault. When someone puffed the breath of life into me, they were a little too enthusiastic; what should have been inside blew out. I imagined it accompanied by the sound of a party horn. Fwip, toot.

Maybe not the goddess of comedy, but tragedy, which can be pretty funny when the Greeks do it. That was Nemesis, I think.

My muscles loosened. My eyes remained closed. Eventually, the water dipped to a temperature of equilibrium and I figured my blankets and sheets would be so much better, if I could just brave the brief bout of chill between here and there. I stood and toweled off, still un-me. The apartment's heat was working just fine, but it was cold enough to make my penis shrivel right up into the hair around it. I entertained a thought: jumping into the snow, dancing for another ice storm, begging frigid Old Man Winter to make it so cold that the damn thing would pop back in where it was supposed to be in the first place.

I followed my better sense, slipped into some flannel PJs, rolled into the comforter to make it like a cocoon, and slept until I was bored of it.

11

The drive out to Spokane took a couple hours longer than usual. The pass was easy; the county had paid it a lot of time and attention. The rough part was out on the open, fallow fields which stretched for a hundred miles between the Columbia River and the city. With temperatures below freezing and a stiff north wind, the snow was like powdered sugar. For miles at a time, the road vanished by a river of shifting white. I followed a beat-up farm truck part of way, hugging its wake. When it turned—successful on their second attempt—into a driveway, though, I was cast adrift.

More than once, I felt my tires creep over the edge of the pavement and onto the shoulder. Each time, I had to fight the urge to overcorrect and send myself sailing across the other lane, or where I presumed the other lane was. During the strongest gusts, I slowed to a crawl until the chaotic waves gave me enough of a glimpse of the white and yellow lines to hold their position in my mind and get up to a pace that at least registered on the speedometer.

Tense and tired from the concentration, I finally arrived at the hospital. They had moved Victor off the burn unit. He was propped up in bed, waiting for me. His arms and face were still bandaged, but his eyes were open and he flashed me a grin when I walked in. He had enough motion in his hands to raise the TV's remote control and click off whatever had been on the screen.

"About time," he said.

He had been unhooked from all his tubes and wires. With a grunt, he twisted himself around and let his legs dangle over the edge.

"You good to walk?"

"Yeah. They've had me on therapy, doing laps down the halls. You bring some clothes? They charge extra if you take their gowns." He tugged at the loose-fitting cotton.

"Looks expensive." Mom had packed a duffle with some things from his old room. I handed it over. He grabbed for it, winced, and lifted it mechanically over to sit on the bed next to him.

Rummaging through it, he grunted. "Feel like I'm in high school again."

I leaned against the tiny sink in the corner of the room, taking a load off, muscles strangely tired from sitting for so long and welcoming the rest.

"Wasn't sure if Gracie still had your stuff. Didn't think to ask her."

"Probably." He let his bare feet touch the tile and put his back into standing. "Unless she tossed it out." He took the bag into the bathroom and pulled the door half-shut behind him.

"Haven't talked to her yet?"

"Nope." I heard a rustling of fabric, and his gown came flying out in a wad. "Shit, none of this would fit me if they hadn't been starving me in here."

"Silver lining, I guess. Hey, do you need me to sign anything?" A sheaf of papers sat on the bedside table, thin yellow sheets from triplicate forms and glossy brochures.

"Better not. They'll be after you next."

"You get an application for charity care or something?"

The bathroom door swung open. If not for the remaining bandages and patchwork puckers of visible skin, I would have thought he was my brother from years ago. His frame looked loose, lanky, held together by wooden pins. The shirt was a favorite brand of his from high school days, the jeans and shoes maybe the only pairs of each he had had throughout his whole senior year.

"Yeah. The nurse brought the discharge papers, and someone from billing tailed her in. All kinds of discounts, since I've got no insurance."

"What's the damage?"

"Pretty obvious. Hey, hit the call light, will you?"

I reached over to the bed and pressed the button for the nurse. A yellow light clicked on just outside the doorway. "That's it, then?"

"Yep. They said they gotta walk us out. You know, make sure they're actually getting rid of me."

Victor stood at the window, hands limp at his sides when I thought to complete the picture they really ought to have been jammed in his pockets. I fetched the duffle from the bathroom, tucked the papers from the table into it, and took a glance around the room for any other belongings.

"Grab the morphine pump, will you?" Victor deadpanned.

"Ready to go?" asked an older lady, padding up to the door on bright, white tennis shoes.

Victor nodded and led the way. I shouldered the duffle and followed.

"We're going to miss having you around," said the nurse, bringing up the rear.

"Thanks."

"Sure you don't want a ride in a wheelchair?"

"No, I'm good."

The nurse followed us to the front door. She hung back in the vestibule as we ducked into the cold. I glanced back once, as I opened the driver's-side door, and saw that she was still watching us. She gave me a little wave, like a lonely grandparent sending off her family after a too-brief visit. Victor didn't spare a second look. Settling in, he buckled up then slipped the shoulder strap behind his back, out of the way.

I pulled out of the parking lot and merged into traffic. "Anything you need to do before we head back? Mom said she's making your favorite for dinner."

He snorted. "What's my favorite?"

"I don't know. Anything but hospital food?"

"Yeah. Hey, stop when you get a chance. I want a beer."

I got us onto the freeway and out of the mild crush of downtown before pulling over at a convenience store. I needed the gas, anyway.

"You got any cash?" Victor asked.

"A bit." I dug a ten out of my purse and handed it over.

"Swear to god, this is the only money I'm taking from you."

I pumped the gas; he bought his beer. The afternoon was burning out fast; it was going to turn dark long before we made it home. The next few miles passed in a wordless rumble of pavement under tires. Victor drank his beer with his eyes closed. He didn't notice me sneaking looks his way. He needed a shave, badly. His upper lip and left cheek had been stitched and grafted, smoothed and ruined, but surviving follicles still sprouted in a mess that reminded me of his adolescence.

When his beer was gone, he crumpled the can and tossed it into the back seat. "How's Jilly?"

"She's fine." I cleared my throat. "Hey, what happened that night?"

He didn't answer at once. I thought maybe he didn't even take the question in. A few more minutes and it would circle back around and just inhabit me. He reached into his pocket, pulled out a folded piece of crisp, white paper, gave it a long look, then returned it. I switched on the low beams, the dusk outside at that stage of equilibrium between light and dark in which everything seems to shade toward blue.

"What's that?"

"Prescription for a couple weeks of painkillers."

"Just a couple weeks?"

"I'm supposed to see a doctor back home for more."

"Oh." I drummed on the steering wheel. We passed through the suburbs, the outskirts, the brief towns that had so far resisted the gravity of the big city. Soon, the wide open fields. At least the wind had died down. I hoped that the road would stay visible.

"Mind some tunes?" I clicked on the radio and let the system auto-scan. This close to Spokane, it found a live station on almost every frequency. We heard five seconds of evangelism, five seconds of country, five seconds of hair metal, five seconds of Spanish as it cycled through. Victor reached up and stopped the scan on a top forty station. A heavy synth beat signaled a block of eighties hits. I'm sure I could sing you the chorus, but damned if I knew the artist's name. "Really?"

"What?"

"I thought you liked hip-hop, is all."

Getting back no taunt, no jibe, I turned to look at him. He was glaring, his browless forehead crumpled downward. Then, without changing his expression, he began to sing in a falsetto along with the radio. He missed a couple words, but soldiered on, putting his heart into it. I cracked up, joined in, made a worse mess of it than he did. We murdered the hell out of that song. And the next.

By the commercial break, I was slowing from fifty to forty to thirty-five, and the road was disappearing under my wheels. The headlights picked up the individual particles in billows of snow, each flake so light that it took barely a breath to send it flying.

"What a shitty year," Victor said, reaching for the lever to tilt his chair back.

"Yeah. Be good when it's over."

"If you see somewhere, I want another beer."

"Nothing for the next fifty miles."

He shrugged, large enough that I could see it without taking my eyes off the road, and sighed himself deeper into his seat. The speedometer showed twenty-five. "Hey— my phone's in the armrest here. Want to give Mom a call and let her know we're gonna be late?"

"Just floor it." He popped open the armrest and dug out my phone. Turned down the radio with one hand, navigating the phone's menus with the other. "What do you have her under?"

"'Mom and Dad.'"

He hit the speed dial. After a couple of rings, I heard Mom's voice, muted. The timbre of her words came through, but not the words themselves. She was worried. "Hi, Mom. It's me. We're fine. Just passed through— what's that one— Creston a few minutes ago. She's got it. Dad would be proud. Yep. At least, I dunno. Probably— yeah more like three. Yeah. Love you, too. Bye." He clicked off the phone. "I'm supposed to tell you to pull over if you feel tired."

"I've been tired for four months straight. I wouldn't get anywhere."

"Just passing it on."

I had to dim the lights as night drew a full, weighted dark around us. The high beams lit the snow too broadly, too vividly, and it looked as if we were warping through a star field. The lower setting torched the road in front of us, a perforated low horizon of the blowing crystals, and then let the darkness have the rest. Much easier on the eyes.

"She hates me." This one wasn't a question, but it lived and died like one in the space between us. "Or, at least, she doesn't really know what to do about loving me anymore."

Victor turned the radio off and puffed air into the silence. I smelled his beer breath. "You know, she thinks it's her fault that you're like you are."

"What? What do you mean?"

"Gotta back up. Ever done the math? What's nine months back from your birthday?"

I ran through the calendar in my head. "March twentieth."

"Their anniversary is the twenty-second. Mom conceived on their anniversary." I thought back to anniversaries I could recall – Dad coming home from work early, Mom putting on makeup from long-unused compacts and tubes, a babysitter coming by for Victor and me. We were usually in bed, supposed to be asleep, when they came back from their date, but I remembered once when I woke up as the door slammed behind the babysitter on her way out.

"Hush," Mom had scolded, then giggled.

The joists creaked softly with the same rhythm we made on Christmas mornings. I climbed out of bed and cracked open the door. Mom, her dress red and shiny and slick, her back up against their bedroom door, a black sweater draped around her shoulders. Dad with one hand slipping in circles higher and higher up her tummy, brushing the lower cup of her breasts. She would never let him get away with that. Then they kissed. Dad slipped the sweater from around her without breaking contact with her lips.

I couldn't decide, at the time, whether I ought to tell Victor. I had decided against it, because he'd probably have thumped me for spying. "Mom was drunk when she got pregnant with me."

Victor nodded. "And she blames herself for how you turned out. Didn't touch another drop until Dad got the cut."

"How do you know?"

"Dad told me about it."

The road ahead for the length of my beams appeared solid, black, and damp. "God, we love to talk in circles, don't we. Me to you, you to Dad, Dad to Mom. Then it breaks down, I guess."

"That ain't how it works."

"Seems like it."

"You're the one who went two years knowing you were trans before saying a word to any of us. That whole time, we knew it. Even Mom, I think, who didn't know the words for it. Two years while your huge silence sat there like a bump on a log." He turned away, facing the window, each of us in the other's peripheral vision. "That's why I was so goddamn proud when you told us. You trusted us. Could have done it earlier, you fucker." The gentle bite of affection assuring me that any hurt from feeling untrusted had been wiped away and replaced with the sort of memory which lingers and informs without barbs or thorns.

"I didn't know."

"I get it."

A fog crept over the road, and a few rapid blinks confirmed it wasn't confined to my eyes. "It wasn't enough."

"Because of Mom? She'll get over it."

"No. Not her. Not just her. I mean— I'm still not me. I mean the biggest change of my life, the deepest unearthing of myself— it still isn't full enough, or deep enough."

"Yeah? Got some recovery time ahead of you?" I nodded a couple of times before I realized he was grinning at me. "Need some painkillers?"

"You offering?"

"Special for family."

I couldn't tell what he was making light of: his condition or his past. And, not super keen on having either suspicion at all confirmed, I didn't ask the follow-up. We passed a landmark of the trip, a grain elevator under which we could still see low piles of unshipped wheat, skinned over with snow.

The first indication I had of the skid was the dummy light clicking on just to the left of the odometer. I had time to wonder, half-aloud, what that strange little amber icon meant before the tires left their bearing and our direction drifted to one side. It's at times like this when your perspective shifts abruptly and the twenty-five we had been managing went from an agonizing slowness to a breakneck swiftness.

"Shit!" I croaked, coughed, adrenaline infusing everything.

"What?" Victor maybe hadn't yet realized.

I steered into the skid and pumped the brakes, calmly focused but expecting that calm to shatter. Four, five, six gentle applications of the pads. The ground split from level and we came to a stop. I unwrapped my fingers from the wheel, killed the radio.

"You OK?"

"Christ." Victor straightened in his seat with a wince.

"Nothing pulled out?"

He shook his head and rolled down his window. I hit the emergency lights and pushed open my door a crack. We had skidded into a trough in the drifting snow, front axle clear but the back had gone buried into a pure white slope. I sat half in my seat and put a slow pressure on the accelerator. The rear tires slipped and whined.

"Rear wheel drive on this thing? Piece of shit," Victor muttered. He reached for his door latch.

"No, I've got it. Here, you take the wheel." I zipped up my jacket and cleared out, leaving the driver's side free. He slid over and positioned his feet on the pedals, reaching down at once to adjust the height and distance of the seat. "Pop the trunk, will ya?"

Victor peered at the dash for a few seconds, trying to find the switch, then punched it with his thumb. The trunk yawned open. Junk, trash, shit, and the emergency kit Dad had prepared for me. Inside, I dug for the Ziploc baggie full of kittie litter. Not a ton, but enough to get under two wheels. First I'd have to clear the snow out of the way, though, and Dad hadn't managed to fit a shovel into the kit.

The road pitch black in both directions, I got down on my knees. I pulled my hands up inside the cuffs of my jacket and stretched, scooped out armloads of powder from in front of the trapped wheels.

"Need a hand?" called Victor, putting one shoe out onto the ground.

"Nope." It wasn't that bad, actually. I felt a bit like a hamster scratching a fresh load of bedding around, using my god-given arms and legs to doze the stuff out of the way. The flakes were so small they melted on contact with my still-hot skin, so numerous that I'd never be able to dissolve them all, and so light that they blew up and down my cuffs and collar.

When I could see through from one wheel well to the other, I stood up, exhaled a few lungfuls of air onto my numb fingers, and fumbled with the litter bag. I used up every grain of the stuff. "Try it." Victor hit the gas, too hard, and spun the tires. "Slower." I stepped into the depth of the drift, closed the trunk, and put my shoulder against the body. Cold slipped like heavy-gauge needles into my feet and ankles, my neck and arms.

He let his lead foot settle on the gas this time, and we picked up enough traction to surge up a couple agonizing inches. I caught the momentum and kept it up, rocking the thing, digging my shoulder in so hard I thought I might dent the body.

"Come on!" Victor shouted out his window. Every time the wheels peaked I thought we had made it out, just to have the ton-and-a-half roll back against me. "Fuck!" I grunted on each worthless shove. Victor hollered out the same on each backward slide. See-saw, back-and-forth, the hot profanity freezing as soon as it left our mouths.

Three times in a row, I thought I had used my last ounce of strength. Then, once more, I dug deep and everything caught: the wheels, my feet, and a long howl of victory from my brother's throat. I fell forward, carried by my own momentum onto all fours. Breathing heavily enough to cloud my vision, I got to my feet and waded back to the road. As I stamped over to the driver's door, Victor leaned out to give me a high-five. It stung like hell.

"I'll take it from here," he offered, nodding me toward the passenger seat.

"You had a beer on top of painkillers."

"Either that or a woman behind the wheel?"

He gave me the widest of all shit-eating grins, even as he twisted himself over the center console and back to the passenger side. In no time, we were back on our way, heater blasting louder than the radio, leaving behind a little dent of nothing on a shrouded landscape.

I turned down the vents once the pins-and-needles had left my fingers and I could feel my pulse returning. We made it off the farmlands and into the foothills, where the wind was buffered by trees. The roads were better, and I picked up some of our lost speed. Victor and I bullshitted off and on, about TV that he had watched and I had missed, about my work, about what it might be like to live on the moon. The further we went, the more he sounded like he was drifting off, but his eyes never shut all the way.

As we started up the pass, he said: "I knew them. The guys that did this to me. They had territory on the other side of the river. Pretty clear boundary. I don't know why they jumped me. I don't know. Drunk, maybe. I didn't cross the river. I saw the fire and the car and thought, holy shit, what's happening. That's all." His forehead rested against the window. He stared through his reflection into the forest, the trees whipping by, dark against dark.

I slowed for a sharp turn. "You fight with them before?"

Motionless, he answered: "No, not those guys. Kept apart." He chuckled, then, and for a second it sounded like something burning. "Remember when I got suspended that one time?"

"Which one?"

"Nah, I only got suspended once. In-house detention, sure, but they only kicked me off campus for that fistfight on the first week of school."

I remembered. I had only witnessed the tail end of the brawl, Victor versus two of the strong native boys. Victor had held his own for a couple minutes, I heard, but two on one didn't make much of a contest, especially considering that the native kids together weighed about three times as much as Victor, and most of that was muscle mass. Wiry and skinny by comparison, Victor could have relied on his quick feet to get away if he had wanted to.

The part I caught started with Victor on the ground on his stomach, one of his opponents kneeling on his thighs while the other gave him a kick across the face. The crowd, all students at that point, spewed so many words that their sum was worthless. I shouted a few along and lost them.

Victor twisted and got one foot free. A kick, weak and savage, landed near the hip of the kneeling boy. Someone laughed; I'm pretty sure it was Victor.

Teachers, coaches, and the vice-principal arrived in quick succession, overwhelming all three boys with numbers and pulling them apart. Victor cussed out loud as the crowd sound muttered off into silence. Then he socked the vice-principal right in the jaw. The fighting on campus, as violent as it was, would have been enough to earn a suspension—and did, for the two other boys—but that punch was it and then some for Victor. He was out for three weeks, and still bore the bruises when he came back to class.

"Damn, I miss that; being a fucking teenager. Getting in trouble, and it stays at the school and home. No god damn FBI or whatever. Who the hell cares. It's my life, and my enemies, and it's all just right here anyway…" His mouth sounded dry, his words aimless. I unscrewed the cap from a bottle of water and passed it over to him. He took a long drink.

"What did you fight 'em for, anyway? Back then, I mean. Drugs?"

He shook his head. "Nah." He took another drink, replaced the cap, and set the bottle between his legs. "You want to make an Indian mad, you shit on his native pride. You want to make a Latino mad, you fuck with his family."

I waited for the angry echoes to subside from his sound and body. "Those would probably work on anyone." Victor shrugged. "I don't want to go back," I said, quiet enough not to make any echoes at all.

"Home?"

"No, to back then."

"Yeah, I believe it. You're better now than you were."

We cleared the pass in silence, slipped across the city limits in silence, arrived home in a cloud of quiet understanding difficult to breathe and impossible to clear.

12

Mom had a roast on warm in the oven when we walked in the door. She gave Victor a slight hug and he bent down to give her a peck on the cheek. "Your Dad's out on a call," she said.

"You eat yet?" Victor asked.

"Waiting for you guys or him, whichever came first." She pulled on her red-and-white checked oven mitts and slid the meat off the tray. In years past, this would be the time when Victor would get the silverware and I would get the glasses, but the table was already set for four. I sat in my old place, Victor in his. He still looked pretty out of it to me, hooded eyes and too-deliberate movements. I caught his glance. "Good?" He shrugged it off.

"Smells great, Mom."

"What would you like to drink?"

"Just water," said Victor.

"Me, too," I said.

Mom brought over two glasses of water, then returned to the kitchen for the platter of carved beef, quartered potatoes, and baby carrots. It wasn't until the first bite touched my lips that I realized how hungry I was. I think I tore through my helping at least twice as fast as the others. I don't know if it was my silence or the sound of my chewing that got to her, but when Mom spoke up she had the tone of someone trying to interrupt.

"And how is Jilly doing?"

I swallowed. "She's fine. I guess I would have heard if something went wrong after the hospital, but it sounded like she was fine before they let her go. Just gave us all a scare."

"She sure did."

"How's Shasta?" Victor asked, a strange little smile on his face. I couldn't guess his motivation, and suspected he wasn't quite sure himself.

"She's OK, too, I guess. I haven't talked to her much for a while."

"You guys still together, or what?"

I chewed another forkful before answering. "We broke up a while back."

He pushed back from the table. "Just trying to keep up," he said. He went into the kitchen and opened the fridge. A moment later I heard the hiss and puncture of a can opening.

"Honey, you should ask your dad about those," said Mom as Victor returned with an open Bud in his hand.

"And your pharmacist," I added.

He took a long pull. "Dad won't mind."

The silence came back, no chewing to fill it, and this time I all but interrupted it myself, but I swear to god I couldn't think of how. Then Mom said: "You need anything else, honey?"

"Nah," said Victor. "I'm just tired." He took that as his cue to head—slow, aimless—into the living room and collapse on the couch, one foot slung over the coffee table. I helped Mom clear up the table. We left a plate out for Dad. On autopilot, I started to fill the sink with suds for the washing up. It had been my chore ever since middle school when Victor had traded mowing the back lawn with me.

Mom took up the place next to me, rinsing and drying.

"You still miss her," she said.

"Shasta?" She nodded, then I did. "I still love her, mom. I don't know, it was never really a two-way street. I took and took and took..." My hands dipped into the water. Looking back, I couldn't believe how selfish I'd been, so damn incapable of seeing that I didn't give anything back.

"She was good for you," Mom said. "I could see it on your face."

"Yes, she was. And I needed that from her, mom, because I might not have made it. I might not have made it through those years without her."

Mom clicked her tongue. "You were strong enough to know you needed something, needed her. That's nothing to be ashamed of."

"But what did I give back to her, what piece of me did I give up to make her better?" I sank my hands into the suds, my fingers now warmer than the dish-water. "And that's what I call love? That scares me, Mom."

"You took on Jilly. You were good to her for that." I shook my head, down at an angle that didn't show her my eyes. When I didn't say anything more, she went on. "Sometimes, things just don't work out. That's how you know God has a different plan. He says to look somewhere else, and you can fight it all you want but the more fighting you do, the more it's going to bring you heartache when you finally realize."

"You think there's someone out there for me."

"Of course there is, honey." She put a comforting hand on the small of my back, not realizing she was dripping wet. "There is a plan, and you'll come to know it. You really will." She touched my hair, then withdrew her hand. She was holding back some part of her opinion, her faith, her certainty. I could tell because I sure as hell was, not sharing that I was certain the universe ran on no plan. A brief flash of irritation at our shared dishonesty burned off and revealed a quiet gratitude. What we shrouded from each other, maybe it wasn't as important as what we let into the light. Maybe the small important truths we shared held more power than the indefinite hidden secrets.

"I haven't run into any true loves in a while," I said with a shrug and a smile to break us out.

Mom returned to the rinsing. "Maybe not around here. Maybe this isn't the place for a person like you." Mom glanced at me and I smiled. "I mean, for where you are in your life. The town doesn't change as fast as you do. Not that it needs to; just that when you change, it doesn't. Jesus couldn't do his work at home. He had to leave to start his ministry."

"Trying to get rid of me?" I grinned at her and for the first time in a long while I saw myself in her features. She flicked water at me from the tips of her fingers. I blew suds at her face.

"Looks like your brother's asleep."

Victor's head had lolled back on the arm of the couch. His mouth had dropped wide open. It looked a bit like he was screaming. "I'll put him to bed," I said.

"I'll finish up here."

It took a couple of good shakes on Victor's shoulder to rouse him. I got a good, front-on look at his face while he blinked and found his bearings. The scars would be with him forever. A slip of a memory from high school English came to me, my teacher explaining that Frankenstein's monster had long black hair, pallid skin, that no he didn't have bolts out the side of his neck.

"Up and at 'em." I pulled Victor to his feet and followed him to our old bedroom, a pace behind. He collapsed onto his bed; I could smell a cloud of scented fabric softener from the freshly-washed sheets. Without a word, he sank back to sleep. I undid his shoes and straightened his legs under the blankets, just barely fitting the twin mattress.

Our room had become a storage space for Mom and Dad. Boxes filled the corners and our old desk had been collapsed and leaned up against one wall. A large tote caught my eye, familiar dust jackets visible through the haze of the clearish plastic. I unclasped the lid and slid it away. Treasuries of children's stories, old editions which Mom had picked up from a library stock sale. I remembered reading each one. It was a summer some time before middle school, some time after I had seen the Disney versions of most of the stories. I remember sitting on the front porch in the shade, drinking water from a big glass jar and wondering when I would get to the happy ending of The Little Mermaid.

I crossed my legs and turned the box so that the light from the hall fell more sharply across the spines of the books. Trailed my fingers over them, reading each title only as I touched it. Robin Hood. Alice's Adventures in Wonderland. Black Beauty. The Frog Prince and Others. I slid the last out from between its neighbors. Fine dust crept into the cracks and pores of my skin. The pages had gone yellow, the illustrations less vivid. I remembered believing so hard that summer that a kiss could break a spell or make one. With no frogs around, I had found a salamander. Its skin had been strangely dry against my lips.

The front door opened and closed with a slam. I returned the book and snapped the lid back on. Victor began to snore as I tiptoed out.

I walked in on Mom and Dad kissing, she holding his bad hand in hers, her small fingers just long enough to encircle his remaining ones.

"Dinner's in the microwave," Mom said as they parted.

"Hi, Dad."

"Hey, kiddo. How's your brother?"

"Sleeping. I'm kind of feeling out of it, too, after that drive. Thinking I'll head home for the night."

"Thanks for picking him up for us."

I nodded, hugged them one after the other, and strode out the door, feeling for all the world like something had just come to an end, but unable to give even myself the evidence to make it mean anything beyond the moment.

13

It was Jeanine who kicked me into gear, as it turned out. Her treatments weren't going as well as her doctors had hoped, so they decided to up the frequency. Rather than drive back and forth to Spokane a couple of times a week, she decided just to sell her house and get an apartment over there. Shasta was working enough to afford a little home for herself and Jilly, so no one really needed that big old place on the orchard.

When Jeanine told me, during another welcome afternoon at Gracie's salon later that winter, I up and said without thinking it through: "Do you need a roommate?" I don't know what possessed me but it felt like an epiphany and I wasn't going to take it back.

"You're serious?" Jeanine asked. I nodded and held my breath. She avoided making eye contact for a moment as the idea tumbled around in her head. Then a smile spread across her face, a slow shining of careful optimism. "Not a bad idea," she nodded.

I grinned back, quick as a flash. We made a plan to go apartment hunting the next weekend. "If you're sick of me after a day of scouring the classifieds, no harm done," I said.

As we left the shop, she gave me a hug. I returned it, but felt as if any pressure at all would crush right through the thin cage of her skin and bones. I imagined I could feel the knuckles of her spine grinding together. She gave me a papery kiss on the cheek. "Thank you."

After that, it was all letters and newspapers and application forms. We found a place we both liked well enough, a ways off from the center of things but clean and with a good park nearby for Jeanine to exercise in. I picked up a job clerking at the hospital where Victor had stayed. When I gave my notice to the administrator at my current job, he asked if I had thought about applying for Joy's position. I declined, thanked them, and said I appreciated the experience and training the place had given me.

My colleagues had a little party for me, passed around a card and filled it up with spider-web wishes of good health, luck, and all the best. Someone ordered in pizza, and Germ came down to share it. We kicked our feet up on the desk and got our fingers all greasy, the brown napkins from the restaurant far too thin to sop up much of the excess.

"Couldn't take this place anymore, huh?" Germ joked.

"All burned out," I replied, matching him tone for tone.

He took one more slice and headed for the door.

That afternoon, I took a break and logged into Flower Chat. I posted a rare message, asking if anyone out there in anonymous land had had any experience with a couple therapists I had looked up in the Spokane area, specialists in gender identity issues. No one had, but plenty of tips rolled in about things to ask during a first appointment, ways to gauge if a given doctor would give me what I needed. Someone wrote: "Be as selfish as you can be with your time together." A couple of responses agreed, a couple disagreed, but it stuck with me.

Mom and Dad were glad I'd found a job before pulling up stakes. Victor thought it was great he'd have a place to crash in the city. Gracie gave me a little scrapbook she had put together showing styles she thought would look good on me. As I flipped through it in her shop, a tear splashed onto one of the magazine clippings, blurring part of a face, words on the backside of the thin paper showing through.

Packing up was no problem. Mom and Dad reclaimed some of the furniture they had loaned me when I moved out on my own, so the only thing of any size I owned was my mattress and bed frame. Dad volunteered to drive it on over to the place in his truck, so that was that. Just about everything else fit into my Camry; the couple of boxes of overflow went into Dad's passenger seat. At the last minute, Mom tossed her marked up copy of *The Joy of Cooking* on top. And that was it.

On a Saturday in late January, I locked up my apartment door behind me and dropped the key into the manager's mailbox.

Dad sat in his truck, the engine idling. "All set?" he asked.

"I have one more goodbye. You want to go on ahead? I'll be maybe a half hour behind you." Jeanine had moved the week prior, in advance of the new treatment regimen, so he wouldn't find the place empty.

He nodded and shifted the truck into gear. As he steered down the road, I could hear the ropes and frames creaking like an old frigate on a final mission out at sea.

◆ ◆ ◆

I drove up to the orchard house. It hadn't sold, yet. Jeanine had mentioned that Shasta and Jilly were still living there, doing whatever touch up work the realtor thought would be best. I parked on the side of the road, crunched up the gravel drive. Decorations that had sat on the porch or hung from the door for years upon years were missing, packed away. I remembered a wind chime made of thin slices of agate, a pint-sized scarecrow holding a welcome sign, a pair of matched wicker chairs. The chime and the scarecrow were gone, the chairs turned to face an unfamiliar direction.

I rang the doorbell. Shasta answered, wearing her pajamas and a pair of yellow rubber gloves. She leaned at once against the door frame, as though exhausted already. "Hi," she said.

"Hi." I paused out of habit, expecting her to carry on with the next step of the conversation. When she didn't, I went on alone. "How are you doing?"

"Pretty busy."

"Sorry. I just wanted to stop by and say I was on my way out of town." Shasta nodded, neck bent down so that even at the height of the gesture she couldn't have seen my face. "Can I say goodbye to Jilly?"

"I'll go get her."

She left the door unlatched behind her, but didn't give me any sign to follow her. I stood on the porch, a cold wave lapping my stomach, as if the winter breeze were passing through all my layers, the false and the true. Jilly's head peeked out into the hallway and I bent to match her posture, my face lighting up and catching hers up with it.

"Hi there!"

"Hiya!" she said. She had on a pair of bright yellow tights, a shirt with a print of Sleeping Beauty, and purple mittens. I came to the doorway and stooped to give her a hug. She caught me around my knees.

"What's with the mittens, kiddo?"

"I'm cold!"

"Uh oh. It's pretty cold, isn't it?"

"I have Aurora on," she said, tugging on the front of her shirt.

"You do! What's she from?"

"I have a make-up on."

She clutched and discarded the topics with such ease. I kissed her on the top of the head. "And you look so beautiful!" Shasta trailed up behind her and tapped her on the shoulder.

"Say bye to Auntie Lita."

"I have make-up."

"Bye, little princess," I said.

"Cold!" She tagged me on the leg, just a little swat, and I couldn't guess why. She ran back down the hall, disappeared into her playroom, giggling and just once letting out a screech.

I stood, finding it easier to hold my smile in place than pull it down. "She wears her mittens inside?"

"It's her thing right now."

"I can't believe how fast she's growing up."

"Yeah."

A gust of wind blew across the porch and encountered no resistance from me. Shasta pulled the door most of the way shut behind her, leaving a crack to listen for Jilly.

"Shasta." My eyes stung. A thousand explanations sprang to mind, each failing to contain completely what I wanted to say, what I wanted her to feel. I pruned them back, quickly and without grace. "I'm sorry," I said.

She sniffed, blinked, met me with eyes as pained as mine. "For what?" Her words came up hard against me, abrupt.

"Everything," I hazarded.

She blew out a short breath. "Whatever."

"OK, you name it, and I'm sorry for it."

"No, you name it! For god's sake." She caught herself, contained her explosion. "I can't just— I'm not your therapist."

"I know."

"You made me feel like my daughter wasn't mine anymore, like you wanted your share and more. Like you were the father you said you never wanted to be. You gave up that right. You gave her up. And then, when you felt like it, you reminded me that you can always waltz right in and steal it back. You don't want that, remember? I don't want you to."

"Shasta, all I am is sorry. I won't invade your life. I'll wait for an invitation. I understand; I really do."

She shook her head. "I know you, Lita. It'll be months before you understand, before you can make your apology mean something."

I wanted to argue. I felt all the indignation pile up in my head, blocking off the tears. Then a blade of something even more pathetic and childish cut through it all. I sighed and put my hands in my pockets. "Can I be selfish on one more thing?"

"What is it?" Our words met at the middle distance, seeming to keep us apart.

"Do you want this?" I withdrew from my pocket a three-by-five picture, one I had found while packing up my apartment. It was a school picture of Simon Hernandez, age fourteen. Drab blue background, awkward pose with arm on a table, too-wide smile because I swear the photographer told a funny joke, pimples, a hint of the same damn mustache that Victor favored. "I don't care who you say it is."

She took the picture, turned it over. There was nothing written on the back. She looked up at me, waited until I met her eyes before asking dryly, "Why?" I shrugged. I didn't have anything to say, to bring to the little battleground between us. My arms opened a little, and she took a step forward. We hugged, but it was formal and graceless.

"OK. Consider me gone." She still used the same conditioner in her hair she had back in high school. The same scent.

"If you're gone, be gone," she said into my shoulder. We disengaged and she slipped back inside without another word or glance. It wasn't until I made it back to my car that I checked to see if she had gotten my coat damp. Just a little bit.

For as long as I could, I sang along with the radio. An hour or so out, I passed into a dead zone between stations but left the static on. It brushed me clean, setting my mind white. The signal that returned was unfamiliar, and I didn't recognize any of the songs. I turned the volume up and made do guessing at the lyrics.

14

S hasta was wrong. It took me well more than a few months to understand the place I had put her in, the stress I had imposed on her. Time passed, and swept so many things along with it. I ended up with a good therapist who steered me toward a weekly gathering of other trans folks. They called themselves a fringe group, but the fringe was pretty well populated. Back home, I had felt alone in the town because there were no people like me. Here, I felt alone at first because there were so many, and they were so much further along. I had to race to catch up.

Jeanine's new treatments were especially rough on her. When she wasn't at the hospital, she was rooted to the couch or bed in our apartment. We had plenty of time to talk, even if I did most of it. She ended up hearing every dull detail of my new work on tracking documentation deficiencies, every crush that flared up, every joke I overheard and repeated imprecisely.

Maybe I over shared. I asked her once, and she replied: "If you run out of things to say, just say so."

Whenever Shasta came to visit I took off, easy and without friction. I missed her, sure, but really I had been missing her since the night of her party way back in high school, so I managed. And I didn't really want to hear about the guy she was seeing. So it was a stale hurt.

A couple of times after the move I got calls from collection agencies wanting to hit me up for Victor's hospital bill. After declining both times, I asked Jeanine about it.

"You're not obligated unless you volunteer."

I resolved to get irritated the next time they pestered me, but that was it. I mentioned it to Dad on the phone during one of our infrequent calls.

"Your Mom and I worked something out with them. Don't worry about it."

As threatened, Victor did come and crash on our couch once in a while. Each time, though, I barely saw him except for when he was asleep or hungover in the late morning. He spent most of his time out with friends. He had dropped a lot of weight and always seemed to be cold, hunching around the cups of coffee I made for him.

On the morning after one of her courses, Jeanine hobbled over to him with no small effort, nausea passing over her face, smelling of night sweat and urine, and said, "You look like shit." He didn't stay with us anymore after that. When I asked him on the phone some time later how he was doing, he said: "Fine."

I asked Mom the same, and got the same back. When I asked Dad, he said, "He's doing OK." Turned out to be an addiction to painkillers. It landed him in the hospital back home more than once. I came to visit during his recovery the second time. We ended up sitting together on the couch watching crummy action movies the whole time, and I drove back to the city feeling useless. Mom asked me to pray for him. I told her I would.

He cleaned up over the next few months, but I have to give the credit to Gracie. She took him back, or maybe it's more accurate to say that she took him on. I don't know what happened behind the doors of her little house or bedroom. I didn't ask. I did come back to town for a trip to her shop, though, and to show off the progress I had been making. Laser hair removal, more development from the hormone treatment, and some voice coaching. It was a wonderful Spring day, and she left the front door open so we could smell the breeze. At the end of our time, I slid a twenty across the counter for her. She came around to give me a hug, called me "sister." Somehow the bill made it back into my pocket.

◆　◆　◆

After a year in Spokane, Jeanine's doctors asked
her if she wanted to go on with her treatments. They
weren't gaining any ground, and their efforts had laid
waste to her body. Her choice was between an esti-
mate of a couple more months with hospice care, or
a couple beyond that with the therapies ongoing. Just
estimates.

"Can't they be more specific?" I asked her over a
chicken soup dinner.

"I'm wildly unpredictable," she answered. She chose
to end the treatments, and almost immediately life
returned to her features, if not her poise and skin and
bones.

◆　◆　◆

Not even a week after her decision, we got a pair
of invitations in the mail. One addressed to her, one
to me. I opened mine up first before bringing them
inside. I was cordially invited to celebrate the union
of Ms. Shasta Beth to Mr. Someone I Didn't Know.
He was a good-looking guy, and their engagement
picture showed them sitting on a bench in a park with
Jilly on his knee.

"Did you know about this?" I asked Jeanine,
handing her copy over.

"Of course." She smiled. "She wanted to make sure
she spelled your name right."

I helped Jeanine pack. She planned to head down a few days early, to help with the final planning and generally be a mother-of-the-bride. Shasta made the trip to pick her up. It was the first time I had seen her in months. She had cut her hair, and mentioned that her groom was watching Jilly.

"See you soon," she said after closing the trunk over her Mom's luggage.

"You bet."

"Bye."

One, two, three. The morning of the wedding, I felt like driving with my windows down. I only managed it for half an hour before smoke from some distant wildfire started giving me a headache. Even with the windows up and the vents closed, I could smell it.

The ceremony was indoors, thank goodness, in a church and everything. The sanctuary was about two-thirds full when I arrived. I saw some faces I recognized from school, one or two from my old job. "Bride or groom?" asked a tall young man in a tux.

"Bride."

He handed me a program and steered me to the pew. I sat by strangers. Everyone was all smiles. I leafed through the program. The wedding party was unbalanced, two bridesmaids and four groomsmen. The maid-of-honor was the groom's sister, the other maid a cousin of Shasta's from the coast. Jilly was the ring bearer and the flower girl, and I tried to guess whether she had demanded both the roles or had them forced upon her. I had my suspicions.

The ceremony was pleasant and short. Jilly wore a pale pink dress, and only deviated from her route once to wave to Jeanine and run for a hug. We dearly beloved were gathered, led in prayer and in song. The couple had written their own vows. They came out in a call and response, Shasta's voice closer to the mic. Trading lines, on beyond three, four, five.

Then they spoke the last line in unison: "I promise now to love only you forever."

Forever. Forward and backward in time. If any words are magical, I hoped some of these were. Then there was kissing and the recessional, a piece of classical music I didn't recognize. In the receiving line, Jilly gave me a hug then snuck between my legs on a wild hunt for a cookie or juice. I watched her weave through the crowd. Shasta touched my arm, then welcomed me in a hug, all lace and perfume.

"Thank you for coming," she whispered.

"I'm glad you invited me." I waited to say it until I could see her eyes again. I shuffled ahead to make room for the next in line. The groom gave me a warm handshake and gripped my elbow with his free hand.

"Thank you for coming," he said.

"I grew up with Shasta," I said, returning the handshake. He nodded, smiled, and released me. I grew up with her, but not quite as fast as her, I thought. I stepped out of the flow of guests, lost in a little eddy of my own. I checked the program. The reception was being held at the community hall nearby, the same place I had gone for Jimmy King's memorial. Hors d'oeuvres and an open bar.

I went on ahead, not nearly the first to get there, and stood in line at the bar for a bottle of water. Staking out an empty table, I sat and waited. The cavernous room bubbled up with laughter, clinking glass, and conversations long before the tables were filled. When asked, I smiled openly and gestured that the seats around me were free. The lights were low, incandescents through patinaed shades. Each time the big double doors opened, the building exhaled.

When Shasta and her man arrived, we all got to our feet and cheered. They cut the cake, resisted the temptation to smear frosting on each others' faces. The DJ passed around a cordless mic for speeches. Applause, which I've always thought was such a smooth sound for being composed of such staccato motions. The first dance, which Jeanine cut into on the second chorus for a chance to hold on to her new son-in-law. Shasta finished out the song with her new father-in-law.

The music went on from saccharine to sinful, and
the dance floor opened up to anyone and everyone.
I'm a wretched dancer, but I wanted to move, and if
the hot, stuffy air was going to choke me out I wanted
at least to give up my breath for part of it. I moved in
the crowd and with it. Shasta left the floor to have a
bite, and when she came back I found her next to me.
I hadn't worn heels, but my shoes were killing anyhow.
I slipped them off. Shasta lifted up her princess skirts
in fear of tripping.

"I love your nails—" I said, catching a kicked-up
glimpse of her pink toes, right at the same time that
she said: "Oh, look at your nails," getting a first look
at my so-purple-they're-black pedicure. She laughed,
sweet breath, and leaned in so I could hear her. "Jinx!
You owe me Coke!"

We spiraled away from each other, lit up in strobe,
a series of still images. I lasted two more songs, then
retrieved my shoes and waited for another bottle of
water. The DJ interrupted the music for the bouquet
toss. From across the room, Jeanine gave me a frantic
gesture to join the crush of women tensed and ready
to spring. I shook my head, but cheered on for the
countdown and the mad dash following. I didn't recognize the girl who came up grinning with the stems
in her fists.

I made my way toward the door and stood there
next to the gift table, taking deep breaths inward every

time the room breathed out. Packages and cards, all silver and gold, had been stacked without much care. It took a few seconds of poking to find my present, a little heart-shaped box with a gift card inside. I slid the package out so it would be a bit more visible.

Another breath. I opened the door, the rush of cold air instantly making my fingers tingle.

3 1901 05909 3015

CPSIA information can be obtained at www.ICGtesting.com
Printed in the USA
LVOW13s1830050114

368161LV00004B/12/P